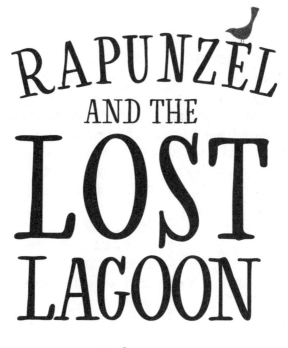

RAPUNZEL
AND THE
LOST
LAGOON

BY LEILA HOWLAND

First Hardcover Edition, September 2017
1 3 5 7 9 10 8 6 4 2
FAC-020093-17202
Printed in the United States of America

Designed by Kurt Hartman

Library of Congress Control Number: 2017936307

ISBN 978-1-4847-8723-6

Reinforced binding

Visit disneybooks.com

For Henry, and all of our adventures ahead
—L.H.

PART ONE

1

RAPUNZEL

"All right, Pascal. If I can get just a little higher, I'll have the perfect view to paint," I said as I hooked my leg over the tree branch.

If my hair were still seventy feet long, I'd use it to climb this tree, probably reaching the top branches in seconds. But now I had to use my legs. I jumped up and caught a low branch, then pulled myself onto it. Slowly and steadily, I stood up. Pascal, my pet chameleon—who was perched on my shoulder and clinging to my neck for dear life—let out a small gasp.

"It's okay, Pascal! I've got you! And anyway, since

when are you afraid of heights?" I teased. Pascal groaned—after all, we'd spent nearly eighteen years in a tower—but out of the corner of my eye I could see his little grin. I balanced on the tree branch, reaching for a leafy bough above. As I stretched up I felt myself wobble, and Pascal tightened his grasp.

"Whoa!" I said with a laugh as I teetered for a second before grabbing hold of the branch, feet dangling. Pascal yelped. "No way am I turning back now, I've waited all day for this moment."

I truly had. I'd felt so out of place all day in my new role as princess, and I was hoping painting an inspiring view would be just what I needed. The castle guards my dad had instructed to follow me everywhere didn't help me feel any more at home. I pretended not to see them watching me as I pulled myself up.

"Wow," I said when I found the perfect perch. "It's beautiful!"

The landscape unfurled in front of me like a dream come true: distant mountains, rolling green hills, and a winding river that glinted in the sunlight.

As I reached for my brushes and paint, Pascal tugged on my newly short hair. "Oh, no! I forgot my sketchpad?" Pascal nodded. I'd been so focused on getting out in the fresh air and painting that I'd actually forgotten the paper! Pascal looked a bit relieved and pointed at the ground. "Okay, fine, but we're coming back up here as soon as I get it!"

I carefully sat down on the branch and swung my legs over the side of the big limb. The first thing I saw when I looked down was my new shoes—the ones I'd kicked off as soon as I'd gotten outside. They were the most uncomfortable shoes ever. Within seconds, the bevy of guards rushed toward me, one with a ladder under his arm.

"I'm okay! I'm okay!" I said. "Really. I can get down on my own."

"Princess, we can't take any risks," a well-meaning guard said as he leaned the ladder against the tree, two other guards securing it with a firm grip.

"Um, thanks for the option, but I was actually looking forward to jumping," I said with a smile.

Before they could protest, I did it. Pascal shut his eyes tight as I leapt to the ground and landed, as always, on my strong bare feet.

It was my first week in Corona and I was still getting used to all the changes. Having so many wishes come true at once was exhilarating. I had parents now. *Actual parents* who adored me and cared for me! Not to mention true love with Eugene—sweet, funny Eugene! Oh, and then there was my new home, the stunning castle with its meringue-shaped turrets and lush gardens. And yet something wasn't right. Something was missing. I was hoping painting would help me find whatever that was, or at least help me end the afternoon on a happy note.

All day, Friedborg, my mom's lady-in-waiting, had been teaching me royal manners. Mom had explained that Friedborg was helping me only until I had a lady-in-waiting of my own. I didn't think I needed one. Up until now, I'd taught myself everything, including advanced astronomy! But I was starting to realize that princesses have to do everything differently.

Earlier, Friedborg had spent hours instructing me on how to sit down properly. And then we'd spent the rest of the day practicing how to open a door. I wanted to do my best, but I was struggling to even have a conversation with Friedborg, since she's not exactly a big talker.

"So I guess you're to show me how to sit?" I asked with a tentative grin as she stood in front of me, pointing to a chair.

She gave me an abrupt nod. Then she shifted her skirts, moved her knees to one side, and dropped into the chair as though she had lost feeling in her legs.

"Like this?" I asked, keeping my back extra stiff and lowering the bottom half of my body as if it were completely disconnected from my torso.

She grunted and frowned, then signaled for me to rise.

"Um, okay," I sighed, wondering how sitting down could be such an art. Was I going to have to learn everything from scratch? Would tomorrow's lesson be about how to stand up? What about walking? It was overwhelming to think about everything I needed to know. I took a breath and tried to focus on the positive. Maybe Friedborg could be my friend if I just tried a little harder. I decided to start with the basics. "So which do you like better, vanilla or chocolate?"

She stared at me for a moment as though I'd just asked her something too personal, like what color her bloomers were. *Oh, gosh,* I thought. *I have so much to learn!*

I guessed that she wasn't up for small talk, so without any conversation at all, I practiced standing and sitting until my feet swelled in my toe-pinching shoes. Three hours and two blisters later, not only had I learned how to sit down like a lady, but I also knew how to close a door without ever turning my back to my company and how to properly hold a teacup. Pascal snuck into the room toward the end of the day and just shook his head as if to say, *Manners are overrated.* I had to agree.

I'd landed on the ground in a low crouch, and when I stood up I couldn't believe my eyes—Eugene was there, presenting me with my sketchpad as though it were the most perfect rose.

"Eugene, you brought me my paper! How did you . . . ?"

"I know you well," Eugene said with a smile. "The paints and brushes were gone, and I thought, 'What do you bet my girl is missing this?'"

"Aw, thanks," I said as he handed me the notebook. My shoulders dropped a half inch and warmth flooded my heart. I hugged him. For a split second, I wondered if I had done that properly, but then I remembered it was Eugene, the person I could truly be myself around. Eugene gave the guards a look and they backed off—a bit.

"Do you notice anything different?" he asked,

turning in a slow circle and striking his "handsome man" pose, though he doesn't need to posture. Eugene's warm brown eyes and mischievous smile are irresistible from any angle.

"Hmm," I said, checking him over. "Is it the new shirt?"

"Nope," he said.

"Have those boots been polished?" I asked.

"Well, yeah, but that's not what I was hoping you'd notice," he said.

"Did the barber give you another haircut?" I asked. Eugene had had a royal grooming treatment every day since we arrived at the castle.

"Getting warmer!" Eugene said, lighting up.

"Hmm," I said. "If you're talking about the swoop of your bangs being a little 'swoopier,' then I don't think that really counts as a *change*."

"What do you mean it doesn't count?" Eugene asked. "The steeper swoop totally changes the shape of my face! Adds a touch of sophistication, don't you think? Does the word *debonair* come to mind?"

"Eugene, you always look great. Now, how about I race you to the top of that tree?" I said, drawing a starting line in the dirt with my foot.

"I can't," Eugene said with a sigh.

"Why not?" I asked, raising my eyebrow in a challenge. "Afraid I'll beat you?"

"Never." He winked. "Actually, your dad really wants me to brush up on laws against criminals . . . and the punishments for breaking them. He says it's part of the, er . . . *formal* education I may be lacking."

"Oh," I said, unable to hide my disappointment.

"I can't let your dad down," Eugene said. "Having my face on wanted posters for the past few years still seems to bug him. You would think that bringing home the lost princess would absolve me of all of that forever, but . . . oh, well!"

"Sorry about that," I said.

"*Sorry*? For what? For giving me the chance to spend the rest of my life with you, my most favorite person in the whole world? For sharing this life of haute cuisine and endless spa treatments? For providing me with a suite in the castle? For offering me a future as a prince, seated next to my best friend?" he said, lifting my chin. "I'll study foreign fancies and diplomatic decorum and macro and micro economics—even microscopic economics, if I have to."

"Is that a thing?"

CHAPTER ONE

"I don't think so, but my point is that I'll join a dishwashing club or participate in a meatloaf-eating competition if that's what it takes to make your dad accept me. I couldn't be happier, Rapunzel."

"Good," I said, biting my lip.

"You want a boost?" Eugene asked, nodding toward the tree.

"That's okay," I said, gently punching him in the arm. "You know I love an adventure, no matter how small."

"See you at dinner," he said, grinning at me as he turned to go.

I watched Eugene walk back toward the castle. Why couldn't I be as happy as he was? I wondered. We had everything anyone could ever want. Was there something wrong with me? It was almost like I didn't even know I was lonely when I was in the tower, but everything had changed now. I could feel the places inside me that had been empty for so many years and I wanted to fill them all up. I took a deep breath and resolved to enjoy myself. After all, it was a perfect afternoon, and I was a girl with a pocketful of paint and a sketchbook full of paper.

I decided to approach the guards and ask them for a moment of privacy.

"So, I'm in a garden, one with a big wall around it. . . . Do you think I could just have a half hour by myself?"

They shook their heads, but I noticed the beads of sweat dripping from their foreheads. Under all their armor, they must've been roasting.

"It's such a warm afternoon," I said. "And that fountain in the main garden looks like the perfect place to take a little break. Maybe dip your feet in the cool water? I'm just going to be sitting in that tree, having a quiet moment of reflection. Do a little painting, you know? I bet a refreshing splash would really feel good. Are you sure you can't take just a little break? It would make me really happy to see *you* happy." One of them cracked a smile, and then the others did, too. "Go on! I'll see you in just a little bit." And they left, giving me a precious few moments of privacy.

Pascal rested in the shade below as I quickly made my way back to my perch. I was just about to pull out a brush when I saw her. There was a girl in a small hidden field. I craned my neck. She had some kind of sword or something, and it looked like she was fighting the air.

Who, I wondered, was *that*?

2

CASSANDRA

I t wasn't easy to fence by myself.

You might think otherwise because there aren't any stakes.

I lunged and no one retreated. I struck the air and no one struck back. I couldn't lose, but I also couldn't win. That took some fun out of it. And then there's all the imagining. I had to pretend there was another person there. I was not into playing imagination games. But how else was I supposed to practice until I was the best? Or prove that it was my destiny not only to be in the guard, but also to one day succeed my father as the captain?

I was supposed to be doing needlework with

other ladies of the court. Nightmare. I'd rather shovel sheep dung than mend clothes and gossip. I'd found this hidden spot the week before using my maps of the ancient underground tunnel system. It was about a hundred paces behind one of the far gardens—close enough to the castle that I could go out there often, but remote enough that I didn't have to worry about anyone catching me shirking my duties.

Fencing helped me deal with all of my frustration. My father was driving me crazy.

"I'm ready for the guard and you know it," I'd said the night before at dinner. "Just give me a chance to at least try out."

"No," he'd said.

"On the winter solstice you said you'd consider it," I pointed out, my mouth full of mutton stew.

"Mind your manners," he said, taking another sip from his chalice. "And anyway, that was then and this is now. Everything has changed."

"Because of her," I said.

"The return of the lost princess is the best thing that's happened to Corona," my father said. He raised an eyebrow. "Surely you share in the happiness of this moment, Cassandra. I would expect no less."

CHAPTER TWO

"I guess," I said, looking through the window and gazing out over the arena, where the latest recruits would begin their formal training the following day. I deserved to be one of them. *I bet half of them don't even know how to hold a sword,* I thought as I watched the royal flags flutter in the wind. I resolved to keep training and working as hard as I possibly could so that soon it would be impossible for my father to deny me.

"I'm sorry to cut this conversation short," my father said. His chair scraped the floor as he stood up from the table. "There's a strategy meeting in the great hall. Now that the princess is back, the king wants us to have her covered at all times."

"What?" I said. "If someone chose to invade us right now, no one would even notice because the entire guard is following that girl around."

It was true. Ever since the princess had returned, the whole force was focused on Rapunzel's every move, even if all she was doing was eating a cupcake or making a wish on dandelion fuzz. Did the king think that the nearby nations of Antipe— or even worse, Dionda—wouldn't notice that our borders weren't being securely guarded? That our army was distracted to the point of uselessness because of a girl's sweet tooth and her penchant for glorified weeds? If there was ever a time to attack Corona, it was now. Could the princess, who was no longer a little girl despite the way everyone was acting, really be so naïve? Did she not get the danger she was putting the kingdom in? I opened my mouth to speak, but my father cut me off.

"Have you forgotten that the king took his eyes off of her for a moment eighteen years ago and she was taken?" His voice was even, but the vein at his temple throbbed.

"She was a baby then," I said.

"Well, 'that girl' is the princess of Corona. You're going to have to meet her sometime."

Not if I can help it, I thought.

My father gave me a stern look and shut the door behind him.

Now, at my practice ground, I thumbed through the pages of my training manual. The book naturally opened to the page I'd read the most—the one with the description of the Winged Beast, the warrior move that was guaranteed to get someone in the guard. The only problem was it required more than one person to pull off. Unlike fencing, it was totally impossible to do alone. I sighed and decided to try the shot put. Throwing the heavy sphere a great distance was one of the first requirements for joining the guard, and I was planning on setting a record.

I lifted the shot, assumed the position, and threw it as high and as long as I ever had.

"Aaaah!" a voice cried.

I looked up and saw someone in a tree. She scrambled down after the shot. Even though I was a hundred paces away, I felt in my bones that it was *that girl.*

Rapunzel.

3

RAPUNZEL

O f all the things I was expecting to happen in the garden that afternoon, having a mini cannonball thrown at me was not one of them.

As the black sphere hurtled toward me and landed with a thud in the grass, I stared at it in wide-eyed wonder for a half second and then shimmied out of the tree to inspect the foreign object.

"Whoa," I said to myself as I picked it up, not expecting it to be as heavy as it was. Pascal and I glanced at each other. He shook his head—obviously he didn't know what it was, either. "She's strong!" I said. He nodded. When she'd thrown it, it had seemed as light as an apple. But this was no piece of fruit! It was some kind of weapon, or something for a sport. I tucked it under my arm, and with a lot of effort, climbed back up the tree. I wanted to show the girl that I had her cannonball thing, but she was gone. Totally out of sight. She was strong *and* fast *and* mysterious. Now I really wanted to meet her.

Whatever this is, I'm sure she'll want it, I thought.

The chances seemed slim that I'd run into her, but there was no way I wasn't going to at least try. As soon as I entered the main garden, the guards, who seemed so happy frolicking in the fountain, hurried to put their helmets back on. I waved at them, glad to see how refreshed they looked. They trailed me as I walked back to the castle. I remembered that from my perch in the tree, it had looked as though the girl had been talking to herself. And I realized then that while I'd spent countless hours talking to myself in the tower, I hadn't done it once since I'd arrived home. It had been weirdly familiar to see the girl doing it. *Does everyone talk to themselves?* I wondered. *Even when they live with lots of other people around?*

I had just turned into the main hall when I saw my mother walking toward me.

"Hello, sweetheart," she said, beaming as she approached me.

"Hi, Mom," I said. I was still getting used to the word *mom*. It tasted sweet yet unfamiliar in my mouth.

"How was your afternoon?" she asked. "Did you enjoy the etiquette class?"

"I'm doing my best," I said.

"That's all I can ask," Mom said. She placed an arm around me, and even though she smelled lovely—like jasmine and lavender—I wondered if she felt as awkward as I did. Were we going to keep walking like this, with her hand on my waist, or was I supposed to wrap my arm around her, too? I paused, trying to figure out what to do. Just as I was about to go for a full hug, she took a step forward and we banged heads.

"Oops! Sorry!" I said.

"It's fine," Mom said, rubbing her forehead. "Are you all right?" I nodded. She gestured down the hallway and we started to walk toward my room. "Tell me, what did you learn?"

"I learned how to sit down, close a door, and drink tea," I said.

"That's a lot for one day," Mom said. I scanned her face to see if she was joking, but I couldn't tell.

She smiled at me. "You know you can ask me any-thing, right?"

"Okay," I said. "Why do I have to learn all these rules? Can't I just . . . be myself?"

"Of course," Mom said. Her long dress swished as we turned a corner, passing a huge portrait of one of my ancestors. He appeared to be scowling at me. Maybe if some more cheerful art filled these walls this place would feel more like home. I debated bringing up the idea of my painting murals for the walls with my parents at dinner. "We just want you to feel comfortable in the court," Mom contin-ued. "After all, you're going to be queen someday. You need to know the customs." I felt dizzy. How was I going to rule a kingdom if I couldn't even master the seven steps of a curtsy?

"What's this?" Mom asked, pointing to the can-nonball thing under my arm.

"I was going to ask you the same question!" I said.

"It's a shot, for shot-putting—the sport and mili-tary training exercise. Where did you get it?"

"I found it in one of the outer gardens," I said.

"How unusual. It was just lying around?"

"No. I was up in a tree and saw this girl who looked like she was practicing with it. And then she threw it. I mean, wow. She threw it so far. She's so strong!" A smile spread across Mom's lips. "Do you know her?"

"Cassandra," Mom said with a nod.

"Cassandra," I repeated. It suited her.

"She's the daughter of the captain of the guard," Mom said, her face brightening. "She's such a unique spirit—brave, loyal, extremely knowledgeable. . . ."

"Do you know where I can find her to return this?" I asked.

"In the east wing. When you return it, why don't you invite her for dinner tomorrow night?" Mom asked. "For the Feast of Elodie the Great."

"I'd love that," I said.

"And, Rapunzel, I know you need to be comfortable, but where are your shoes?"

"Um . . ." I looked down at my bare feet and wiggled my toes on the tile floor. I had a sinking feeling that I had just doubled the number of etiquette lessons in my future. "I think I left them outside."

"Shoes aren't the priority right now," Mom said with a smile. "But please bring them in before sundown. I think we need to find you a lady-in-waiting sooner rather than later."

4

CASSANDRA

I returned to my room immediately, hoping that I wasn't going to get in trouble. Not only had I been caught practicing my shot-put skills when I was supposed to be crocheting appliqués or something equally torturous, but I'd been seen by the princess herself. What if I'd scared her? What if she thought I was attacking her? No one had come looking for me yet, but I had to play it safe. Regardless, whatever guards were supposed to be watching her had really fallen down on the job. I thought I'd better lay low until I was sure she wasn't going to make a big deal about this.

Then I saw the note on my desk from my father.

RAPUNZEL AND THE LOST LAGOON

*Friedborg reported that you missed your afternoon
duties AGAIN. Please be advised that this is unaccept-
able. The queen is looking for a lady-in-waiting to serve
Princess Rapunzel. It would be a great opportunity for
you, and you must show the queen how prepared you
are to train her in the ways of the court.*

I crumpled the note and threw it to the ground. A
lady-in-waiting? Me? Ha. Ladies don't wield weapons, lead military strategy meetings, or race on
horseback. Ladies do needlework, flower arrang-
ing, and hairstyling.

My father knew that, and yet he wanted it for
me? A ripple of anger went through me. I had no
intention of babysitting a princess. Luckily, I wasn't
exactly an active member of the tapestry weaving
club.

Sorry, Dad, I thought. *Keep dreaming.*

I opened my weapons closet to hang my sword.
I followed the handbook of the guards to the letter,
so my materials were always in perfect order. The
pocket where I stored my shot was empty. *Ugh.* I
needed to retrieve it, but not until after dark. For
now I was going to focus on finding a new place
to train. How annoying. That remote field had
been ideal. It was flat, spacious, and hidden—well,
except for when there was someone in that tree.

CHAPTER FOUR

I opened the secret drawer inside my closet and pulled out the maps of the kingdom I'd been working on ever since I was little. Corona was huge and held enough secrets to keep a mapmaker busy for a lifetime—unless that mapmaker was me. I was planning on having this land charted in the next year. Except for a few blank spaces and some unknown spots, I was close to having the most comprehensive and detailed maps of all time—closer than anyone else had ever come to knowing the far reaches and concealed treasures of this land. But close wasn't good enough for me. As part of my mission to be a guard, I was going to complete my maps and present them to my father.

I'd already included most of the tunnels, which created an elaborate underground system of pathways. There were the ones built by Herz Der Sonne for the War of Unification, and they were well-documented. They'd been used for military procedures only a few hundred years ago. But there were also ancient caves, dating back thousands of years, and they were way more obscure. Just the previous night I'd read about the faraway land of Yultadore, which had once been a thriving trade city. A few of its caves had collapsed during a great flood, creating mysterious pools in the middle of the country. No one even knew about them until foreign invaders used them as hideouts from which they launched attacks. I couldn't help wondering if Corona had any pools like that. After all, we'd had great floods before. They'd been written about in history books. Our terrain was similar to Yultadore's.

I would not rest until I scoured the entire kingdom. My maps would truly give Corona the power to protect itself against any intruders. I was just about to unroll one of the parchments on the table when there was a knock on the door.

"One second," I said.

I placed the map under my bed, thinking it would be my father, ready to lecture me. But when I opened the door, my eyes went wide. It was the princess, smiling at me like I was holding a birthday cake. I'd avoided her for a whole week, but now I couldn't seem to get away from her. I followed her eyes to the floor. The map had rolled out from under my bed. I toed it back under.

"Can I help you?" I asked.

"Hi!" she said. Her enthusiasm was so shiny and bright I had to squint. "I'm Rapunzel."

"I know," I said.

CHAPTER FOUR

"I have your ball, um, thingy," she said, holding up my shot.

"Thanks," I said, taking it.

"Hello," someone else said, and then her pretty boy, Eugene, peeked around the corner. "Hear you got a strong arm."

"And I hear you have sticky fingers," I said. No one seemed to care that one of the most wanted thieves in Corona was living inside the castle. I did.

"She got you, Eugene!" Rapunzel said with a laugh. Then she turned that high-noon smile back on me. "I haven't met anyone yet who has comebacks quick enough for him. And trust me, I've met a lot of people in the past week."

"Let's not get carried away," Eugene said. "I don't know if one quip qualifies as keeping up with me."

I arched an eyebrow. He winked. *Ugh. Who winks?*

"Thanks for this," I said to Rapunzel. I was about to close the door when she ducked her head inside and stepped over the threshold into my room. The hair on the back of my neck stood up.

"Can you tell me what you were doing with that . . . shot, right?" Rapunzel asked. The thief tried to follow her inside but I blocked the doorway. "Was it a game? Are you on a team?"

"I play *individual* sports," I said.

"Like running?" she asked. "Because I love to run, too."

"Oh," I said. I let the silence get awkward. Maybe then she'd get the hint.

"Anyway," Rapunzel said. "I came by to invite you to dinner tomorrow night, for the Feast of Elodie the Great."

"Thanks, but I'm busy," I said. "My father and I—"

"Guess what? I already checked with him," Rapunzel said. "And he thought it was a great idea!"

"You *what?*" I asked. This girl had nerve, seeking my father's approval without even knowing if I wanted to go or not.

"I asked your father if you two would join us for the feast! I figured since our families work so closely together, it would be nice if we were with each other for a feast day," Rapunzel said. I swallowed hard. She tilted her head. "Will you sit next to me?"

"Hey, that's my seat," Eugene said.

"Eugene, there's a seat on either side of me, remember?" Rapunzel said.

"I sit wherever I'm assigned," I said.

"Then I'll make sure you're assigned to sit next to me," she said.

CHAPTER FOUR

"Thanks." A soldier knows when to make a tactical surrender. Any more resistance and I'd draw attention to myself. "I'll see you tomorrow night, Princess."

"Please just call me Rapunzel," she said, touching my arm. I flinched.

"Okay," I said. "Rapunzel."

"Bye," she said with a little wave.

"Goodbye."

They left and I shut the door. And then I locked it.

5

RAPUNZEL

"Is it just me, or did the temperature in Corona just plunge to arctic levels?" Eugene said when we left Cassandra's room and walked down the long hallway. He was taking me to what he said was going to be one of my new favorite places. "Brrr!"

"What do you mean?" I asked.

"Cassandra is cold as ice!" Eugene said. "As in, a little rude? What do you think?"

"What did she do that makes you say that?" I asked.

After all, Friedborg wasn't exactly a chatterbox.

CHAPTER FIVE

Maybe reticence was the Coronan way? To me she'd seemed cautious and maybe a little reserved. But the determination and spark that had propelled the shot she'd thrown was also present in her eyes, and it made me want to learn what she knew about the kingdom.

"She's just lacking basic friendliness!" Eugene said, taking my hand as we walked past the throne room and turned down a hallway I hadn't noticed before. "You know, like, 'Hi, how are you, nice to meet you. You don't seem like a cold-blooded criminal so I'll treat you like a normal person.' That kind of thing."

"Maybe she just takes a little warming up to. Don't forget, I hit you with a frying pan the first time I met you," I said.

"True," Eugene said, opening a heavy wooden door. "But that was different."

"Wait!" I said, gasping as I took in the room around me with its high ceilings, tall windows, and walls of books. "These are all books?"

"That's right," Eugene said, smiling proudly. "It's called a library."

"Library," I repeated as I stepped inside. "Library, library, library." The word itself sounded magical, like it could be the name of a constellation, or a butterfly with bright wings, or a concert of bells. *Library.* I loved it!

"How did it take me a week to find this place?" I wondered aloud as I climbed a ladder to reach the highest shelf.

"Somehow the library was in the *middle* of my list of things to show you. After the ballrooms, the gardens, and the spa, but before the buttery and the laundry vats—anyway, you're here now, right?" Eugene asked. "Do I still get points for showing you this?"

"Yes," I said, a hand to my chest. "A million! And I don't know where to start!"

"You can take these books back to your room if you want," Eugene said.

"I can?" I said, staring at the stocked shelves around me.

"I think I'll open a window," Eugene said. "It's a little musty in here."

"I love it," I said, marveling. I used to think there were only three books in the entire world: one about cooking, one about geology, and one about botany. I read them over and over again until I'd pretty much memorized them. I was ready for more, but I hadn't expected this. To be surrounded by this many books was like discovering there were hundreds of other moons just hiding somewhere else in the sky.

"But there's so many to choose from!" I said as I climbed another ladder to check out the high shelves. "Seriously, where am I going to begin?"

"Let's let fate decide. Hold on," Eugene said, and before I knew it, the ladder was flying across the room.

"Woo-hoo!" I laughed, the spines becoming a blur until I grabbed on to a shelf labeled ADVENTURE STORIES and brought myself to a halt.

"Now that's more like it! I bet the Flynn Rider books are in there," Eugene said, grinning from ear to ear. Flynn Rider was the brave and daring fictional character whom Eugene loved so much as a kid that he'd actually called himself Flynn Rider until we met. I'd convinced him that his true name, Eugene Fitzherbert, had an originality and integrity of its own. "Do you see them, Rapunzel?"

"Here," I said, plucking *Flynn Rider: Volume One* from the shelf and handing it down to him. I pulled another adventure book, *Elena Evangelo: Queen of the Desertlands*, down for myself and started a pile.

"Ahhh, brings back memories," Eugene said as he settled into a chair by a window and propped up his feet on an ottoman. I continued to search.

I wanted to know more about stars, so I took several from the astronomy section. And of course there were the books about great heroes of Corona. And I needed a bunch of books about Coronan flora and fauna. I wanted to know what I was looking at while I explored! And then there were the cookbooks, with so many recipes I'd never even dreamed of: raspberry linzer torte; ginger pound cake with peach sugar glaze; honeydew ice cream with rosemary syrup! My mouth was watering as I added six cookbooks to my pile.

The mathematics section was next. The books were filled with information about lines, shapes, angles, and something called three-dimensional polyhedra. What was that? I needed to know! My head spun as I scanned the chapters covering fractions, ratios, and permutations. *As an artist I need to understand all this stuff!* I thought. Especially if I wanted to do more with perspective, not to mention sculpture. I pulled out my favorites and added them to my stack.

"Eugene, there's an art section!" I said when I discovered it, my heart just about leaping out of my chest. I turned to him, but his eyes were closed and he was gently snoring. He had a big smile on his face, and I imagined that's what he looked like as a little kid, dreaming about Flynn Rider. I let him take his nap. I was going to be there a while.

I sat down on the floor, made myself comfortable, and pored over the books for hours. The volumes were big, heavy, and colorful, with glossy pages that I wanted to hang on the walls of my new room. I'd always thought of art as something that was experienced rather than studied, but in front of me were at least a hundred books about color, technique, and the history of the greatest artists of all time. Drawing with ink; sketching with charcoal; painting landscapes, still lifes, and portraits; ceramics, weaving, and crafts! My stack of books was as tall as I was!

When I saw that the sun was beginning to set behind the window, I knew it was time to meet my parents for dinner. But before I woke Eugene, I decided to pick out a book for Cassandra. I could give it to her the next day at the Feast of Elodie the Great.

I looked for something about sports for her—individual sports. I spotted a book called *Field Sports: The Complete Guide*. It covered the history of field sports, technical instruction, and strategy, and had detailed illustrations. I was about to add it to my pile when I noticed there was another book behind it.

It looked like it had fallen there by accident. It was thin and a little smaller than the other books but eye-catching because of its faded green leather cover and the gold edging of its pages. I opened it and coughed at the dust that floated from inside.

The title was printed in thick black ink with gold flecks: *The Lost Lagoon.*

I turned another page to discover this was a book of poems. It had nothing to do with sports. It had obviously slipped into the wrong section—or perhaps it had been hidden? The first poem was called "The Lost Lagoon," just like the title of the book. Half of it was written in English; the other half was in a language I didn't recognize. I spoke the words aloud and they made a kind of music:

> "'When on a winter eve we met, our truth
>   was but a glimmer.
> The moon shone extra bright; fortune far
>   beneath did shimmer.'"

Maybe this book would inspire a new work of art! I didn't know what form it would take, but the mystery of the creative process was part of what made me love art so much. The sun was dipping below the hills and the sky turned from orange to indigo. I gripped the book in my warm hands as a cool breeze billowed the drapes.

It was time to go, but this book was coming with me.

"Eugene, we should go to dinner," I said, sitting beside him and shaking him gently awake.

"Wow, that's a lot of books you picked out!" he said as he sat up and rubbed his eyes. "You realize we have the rest of our lives to use this library, right?"

"Yes, but . . . I don't know, one book just kind of led to another!"

"Maybe you'll need some bookshelves in your own room," Eugene said.

"Like my own private library?" I asked.

"Exactly," he said. "We'll talk to the royal carpenter about it. But for now, maybe let's just take your top ten?"

"Eleven," I said, tucking the small green book in my pocket.

Later that night, after dinner with my parents and a stroll with Eugene in the gardens to retrieve my shoes, I settled into my bed with the poetry book.

I had just opened it when my mom knocked on the door.

"Sweetheart," Mom said, poking her head in. "Are you awake?"

"Yes," I said. Instinctively, I tucked the book inside my covers, though I'm not sure why. I just wasn't ready to share it.

My mother entered my room, beamed at me, and sat down next to me on my bed. She took my hands in hers. "Darling, the time has come for me to assign your lady-in-waiting."

"Already?" I asked, sitting up a little straighter. "I mean, I know I had a rough day today, but I can try harder."

"A lady-in-waiting isn't just someone who helps you," Mom explained. "She's a constant companion."

"But I have Pascal for that," I said.

Pascal smiled up at Mom from a nearby ottoman. Truthfully, I wasn't sure what I would do with a constant *human* companion. I was pretty good at entertaining myself.

"I know," Mom said. "But you have an awful lot of occasions coming up. You're a princess now. I really think you'll need someone to help you navigate these sometimes tedious but necessary ceremonies, and to be your friend and confidante."

CHAPTER FIVE

"I know I can handle it, Mom," I said.

"You have a responsibility, Rapunzel," Mom said. "To this kingdom. And as much as I love Pascal, you need a guide." I felt her words like a weight. I wasn't ready to hear about responsibility—I was just learning to live in more than one room! And yet her eyes were full of kindness and truth. "The entire kingdom has been awaiting your return. Do you understand?"

"I think so?" I said.

"Good. I've decided to appoint Cassandra," Mom said.

"The captain's daughter?" I asked, though I doubted there could be two Cassandras in the same kingdom—at least, not if one of them was the girl I'd met today.

Mom nodded with an easy smile.

"Okay," I said. I remembered the strength of her throw and the fire in her eyes. Maybe having a lady-in-waiting wouldn't be so bad if it was her. "Okay."

"Cassandra is a wise and brave girl," Mom said. "She knows the ways of the castle and how this kingdom works."

"I see that," I said.

"I know you do," Mom said.

"Cassandra is my lady-in-waiting," I said, smiling to myself as I imagined her teaching me how to throw a shot or handle a sword.

"Perfect," Mom said.

"Yay!" I said.

"You can announce tomorrow at dinner," she said, kissing my cheek. "Until then, it's our secret."

After she left, I pulled the book out from under my covers and tried to read the next poem. The words were foreign, but I decided to speak them aloud anyway, and as I did they made a kind of music. When I closed my eyes I wondered what it would be like for Cassandra to be my lady-in-waiting. Would she teach me her warrior moves? Would she tell me everything she knew about Corona? Would she eventually be a little friendlier?

I took several deep breaths and at last drifted off to sleep. That night I dreamed of water, and of a secret that swam like a silver fish inside it.

6
CASSANDRA

"There you are," Queen Arianna said as I tried to slip into the dining room unnoticed. I'd never felt at home in ladies' gowns. Whenever I donned layers of tulle and silk, especially with my hair pulled back into a bun, I felt like I was playing dress-up.

"Good evening," I said, and curtsied.

"I saw you riding Fidella this afternoon," she said.

Fidella was one of the great horses of the kingdom—strong, fast, and highly intelligent. She was matched only by Maximus, a regal and handsome stallion. They were the horses I loved to ride most.

"She's an excellent horse," I said.

I'd been up most of the night studying both my own hand-drawn maps and all the other maps of Corona I'd collected over the years. It was time for me to get even more serious about filling in the blanks, not only so I could prove to my father how essential it was that I be in the guard, but also because the new princess was distracting Corona's line of defense. Others could take their eyes off the ball. Not me. With Fidella I was able to cover a lot of ground, but I hadn't found anything remarkable. I'd have to try again the next day.

"And you've become a skilled rider," Queen Arianna said. "I'm impressed. I also know how dedicated you are to keeping Corona safe."

"I am," I said, chin up.

"I have some news tonight that I think will really please you," the queen said. She winked at me and then went to greet the king. *What is it with winking these days?* I thought for a quick moment before another, much more exciting idea popped into my mind.

My father might not want to reward my training and military acumen, but that didn't mean the queen didn't.

CHAPTER SIX

"I made sure that your name card was next to mine!" Rapunzel said as I approached the table.

"Great," I said, my mind still focused on the queen's words. Was it possible that she would give me the chance to try out for the guard? I stared at the floor to discourage Rapunzel from trying to make any more conversation. That's when I noticed Rapunzel's feet were bare. Here? In the royal dining room? On the Feast of Elodie the Great? What was she thinking? If there were to be an intruder, she couldn't run for cover fast enough with bare feet. What if she stepped on broken glass? *The queen would not regret putting me on the guard,* I thought, though I had to admit that my own feet were throbbing in my formal shoes. I really hated heels.

"Hi there, sport," Eugene said and clapped me on the shoulder. The sound of his smooth voice made my blood turn to ice water.

"Don't call me that," I said. He was smiling at me, but I could tell he'd rather I got lost. Too bad. I was onto him. If he had any plans to run off with the crown jewels, he could forget about them. I was watching.

"Nice to see you, too," Eugene said.

"Hey, have you ever been to the library?" Rapunzel asked.

"No," I said. Everyone was getting settled and chatting, but I wanted the feast to get under way. My palms were sweating. When was the queen going to make her announcement?

"I love it," Rapunzel said. "I was there yesterday for hours and I couldn't believe all the books! I found this one book of poems. The cover is made of the softest leather and half of the book is in a different language—it's charming and romantic and mysterious and complex...."

"Not into poetry," I said.

"But have you ever read a book about ... sports?" Rapunzel asked.

"Huh?" I said.

She grinned as she handed me a book titled *Field Sports: The Complete Guide.*

"Uh, thanks," I said, giving it a quick once-over and then placing it under the table.

The queen touched Rapunzel's shoulder and knelt beside her.

"So," Eugene said, distracting me. "What's it like to be the daughter of the captain of the guard? You obviously have a thing for weapons."

CHAPTER SIX

"So," I said.

"Have you been training since you were a little kid?" Eugene pressed on. "Do you have friends in the castle?"

"No," I said. "Who needs friends?"

"Jeez!" Eugene muttered while Rapunzel whispered with the queen. "I don't need just any icebreaker here, I need a pickax."

I rolled my eyes.

At last the king tapped his glass. He and the queen stood up. The chatter quieted as we gave them our respect.

"We are all here now," King Frederick announced, lifting his chalice. "Let us offer thanks for our bounty and wish one another peace."

Everyone clinked their glasses and said, "May we have peace."

I spoke the words along with everyone else, but deep inside I just wanted to get to the point: I was joining the guard. Right?

The well-wishes and peace offerings seemed to go on for an eternity. At last Queen Arianna spoke. "On this happy occasion, our family is delighted to make an announcement that I know will be nothing less than providential." The queen turned to me and I sat up tall. My breath grew shallow in anticipation. "Rapunzel, would you please do us the honor?"

"Yes," Rapunzel said. The queen nodded and smiled. Why would Rapunzel announce my invitation to join the guard? She turned to me, and her face was suddenly way too close to mine. I pulled back. "Cassandra, I'd like you to be my lady-in-waiting."

"What?" I asked quietly. For a moment the world blurred, and there was a buzzing in my ears. Had I really heard that? Was it true? This couldn't be real.

"You're my lady-in-waiting! Isn't it wonderful?" Rapunzel asked. Everyone around the table was clapping, my father loudest of all. The only one who wasn't grinning like an idiot was Eugene.

"Cassandra, what an honor," my father said. I reached for my chalice of water. My mouth was totally dry. "Congratulations."

"This is a most fortuitous union!" Queen Arianna said. I couldn't form a response. "You can begin your duties tomorrow. Though, really, your first job will be to get to know our dear Rapunzel."

"May I be excused for a moment?" I asked.

CHAPTER SIX

I walked out of the room, sucking air so I wouldn't scream, and then ran down the hallway, my footsteps echoing off the walls.

"Move it," I said to the guards in front of the eastern door. They looked at me quizzically—like I wasn't making sense. "I said, move it!"

They jumped aside. I banged out the door, tore off my horrible shoes, and ran toward the forest. My stomach twisted. My heart thudded. My thoughts raced. I slowed when I reached a thicket, caught my breath, and leaned against the trunk of a giant oak.

How could the queen think this was the best use of my talents? She had just praised my riding ability and—I *thought*—my promise as a defender of the kingdom. My father must have known this was coming. He more than anyone knew I wasn't cut out to sew buttons on dresses or teach manners. And yet here I was, doomed to babysit the world's peppiest princess.

How was I going to train? How was I going to live the life I was born to live?

Fury heated my blood as I stared down the moon.

My pet owl, whom I simply called Owl, swooped

down from above. No matter where he was, he could always sense my distress and would fly to my side as quickly as possible.

"There's nothing I can do," I said to him. He circled the trees above, hooting.

This was a decision that had bars around it. I couldn't protest without falling out of favor with the king and queen, and then there would be no way I'd ever be allowed in the guard. I couldn't argue my way out of this with my father. A royal assignment was the final word. My fate had been sealed. I fell to my knees and stifled a scream.

7

RAPUNZEL

"Are you sure this is the right move?" Eugene asked me as I tidied my room in anticipation of Cassandra's arrival. I wanted everything to be perfect for our first official princess and lady-in-waiting get-together. It was the evening after the feast, and I'd made cinnamon cookies from a recipe in one of the Coronan cookbooks I'd found in the library. There was a whole stack waiting for her, along with a pot of piping hot peppermint tea. "Are you sure Cassandra is the right girl for the job?"

"Of course," I said, turning to face Eugene, who was lounging on the daybed, eating a cookie. His brow furrowed. I put a hand on my hip. "Why? Are you worried? I've never been so sure—except about you!"

He glanced up and smiled, color filling his cheeks. "Aw, thanks," he said. "It's just that Cassandra's a little stiff. Tougher than bison jerky, to be specific. Don't you think?"

"I prefer the word *strong*," I said, fluffing the pillows on my bed.

"She thinks she knows everything," Eugene said.

"Confidence is always appealing," I said, and straightened the blankets.

"She's impossible to have a conversation with," Eugene said.

"More like . . . contemplative. Look," I said, stacking my books from the library into neat piles. "Let me tell you what I see in her. I see a great adventurer. A girl who isn't afraid to explore and try new things."

"And insults," Eugene said.

"She was just teasing you," I said, taking a seat next to him. "Maybe you two are too much alike. You love to tease, too!"

"Ugh. I just get the feeling that she doesn't like me," Eugene said.

"Who couldn't like you?" I asked, brushing his hair out of his eyes. Again he blushed, and it filled me with affection. "I think you both just need some time to get to know each other. You're amazing. She's amazing. I mean, did you happen to see that map she rolled up so quickly when we knocked on her door?" Eugene shook his head. "It was all kinds of amazing."

"You're the amazing one," Eugene said, staring at me with adoration.

Just then there was a tap on the door.

"Oh, that's her!" I said, clapping my hands. "Eugene, I adore you, but I think you should leave."

"Really?" he asked. "But what about our nightly stroll?"

Cassandra knocked again.

"One second!" I called, and then I took Eugene's hands in mine. "I think it's better if my very first meeting with Cassandra is just the two of us. It doesn't mean that she's more important than you or that we won't be taking anymore evening strolls, okay?"

"Okay," Eugene said. "I guess I have some diplomacy reading to catch up on. Your father wants me to be versed in the ways of the court as quickly as possible. And my energy is flagging, so I'll take one of these treats for the road. . . ."

I handed him a cookie, gave him a squeeze, and then opened the door. When Cassandra saw him, her face clouded over like a stormy afternoon.

"I'm just on my way out," Eugene said, and shot me an *I told you so* look. "Have fun, ladies."

"Hello!" I said, giving Cassandra my warmest smile.

"Hey," she said, straight-faced.

"Welcome, Liw! Get it—lady-in-waiting? Liw? Can I call you that?"

"No," she said.

"Okay," I said, shaking it off. "Look. I have cookies and tea for us." I offered her a seat in one of the plush chairs.

"Thanks. I don't eat sweets," Cassandra said.

"I honestly think you're going to love these cookies," I said. "I made them from this Coronan cookbook. It says they're a classic crowd-pleaser?"

"Fine," Cassandra said, and even though she was trying to hide it, I think she kind of liked the cookie.

"I want to start by saying I'm just so excited! When I saw you out there in that field, I just had to get to know you. And when my mom suggested that you be my lady-in-waiting, it felt so right to me. Do you know what that's like? When something just feels right?"

Cassandra stared, taking another cookie.

"Anyway, according to this book, a lady-in-waiting's duties include teaching me manners, languages, and dances prevalent at court; reading and composing correspondence—though, honestly, I don't know who's going to write me a letter; painting, which I love with my whole heart; horseback riding—sign me up!—music and participation in other queenly pastimes. There's also care of my wardrobe—I'm not too into clothes, so let's not worry about that; matters of diplomacy; supervision of servants; keeping me informed about everything that's happening at court; and discreetly relaying messages upon command. But I'm not exactly the type to give commands. I guess you could say we have a lot of work ahead of us."

Cassandra had placed the cookie on her lap and was growing paler by the second.

"You know what," I said. She seemed as overwhelmed as I was by all this castle business. "Let's change the subject. This is the book I was telling you about." I picked up the small green book and opened it to the first poem, "The Lost Lagoon."

"It's in two languages, so I don't understand every word, but the first part is all about this ancient power. Then the poet writes about these ancient caves that the rain opened up with a million tiny kisses. Isn't that beautiful?"

"Ancient caves?" Cassandra asked, her eyes growing wide.

"I'll just read it to you," I said. "Here goes. 'The Lost Lagoon.'

"'When on a winter eve we met, our truth
    was but a glimmer.
The moon shone extra bright; fortune far
    beneath did shimmer.
Here was Corona built, amidst ebbing fear
    and flowing doubt.
When voices clash and metal strikes, the
    light within tamps out.
Ancient caves collapsed, their ceilings filled
    with swaths of sky;
Beneath pooled the water, dear. We entered it
    with lack of fear.
Truth was sealed in precious stones—they
    hold the ancient power
That underlies Corona's strength and binds
    us like sun to flower.'"

"Precious stones? Ancient power?" Cassandra asked, leaning in.

"See, I knew you'd like poetry! Don't you just love the imagery?"

"Keep reading," she said.

"There's something in another language. . . ."

"That's Saporian," Cassandra said, startling me with her enthusiasm. She was standing behind me now, reading over my shoulder. "This book is really old."

"What do you mean?" I asked. "Wait. How do you know?"

"Hundreds of years ago, Corona was two different lands—Old Corona and Saporia. The fact that this is written half in Saporian means that this book is genuinely ancient. No one speaks Saporian anymore except a few scholars."

"Really?" I asked, intrigued. "I'd like to know more about the history of Corona. Can you teach me that?"

"The kingdom's blacksmith, Xavier, is the real historian. He knows everything," Cassandra said.

"Do you think he could give me lessons?" I asked. My pulse sped up as I realized there was so much to find out about my new home. Maybe by learning about it I would, somehow, become more a part of this place.

"Probably. Keep reading," Cassandra said.

"Okay," I said. Cassandra paced as I read: " 'Where the two oaks grow close, roots weave like fingers. Hands clasp together; in spaces between, truth doth linger.' I just love that line!" I said, a hand to my heart.

"Continue," she said.

" 'Berries shine in dew like rubies,
  outstretched arms guide seekers west.
Three divisions bring three decisions;
  remember, hearts know best.
Moonstone, topaz, opal; the emerald tapestry
  does unfold.
Tread lightly to the lost lagoon, holding
  treasures vast, untold.'

"Then it goes on some more in what I guess is Saporian," I said. "Doesn't it feel so alive? Do you think it's real?" Cassandra grabbed the book in her hands and flipped through its pages. I sat up a little straighter. "Hey, maybe we could start a literature circle." I took in her wide eyes. "Wait a second, do you know something about this place?"

"No," she said, fixated on the text. "Is there anything else about caves?"

CHAPTER SEVEN

"Um, does this have anything to do with those maps?" I asked.

"What maps?" she asked, continuing to read.

"The ones I saw in your room." Her head snapped up. "Cassandra, what is it?"

"Nothing. I'm a little tired," Cassandra said.

"You don't look tired," I said.

"I am. What do you say we call it a night?"

"Really? Now?" I asked.

"Yeah. Now." She yawned, but it wasn't very convincing.

"Well, I guess I *am* kind of a morning person," I said as she nodded and tucked the book in her pocket. "So, do you . . . want to borrow that?"

"Yup," she said, and before I could hug her good-bye, she was out the door, clutching the book.

8
CASSANDRA

I ran back to my room, lit my lantern, and unrolled my maps. I'd seen enough ancient documents to know that this book was from several hundred years ago. I had mapped the old-growth trees and knew there was a pair of twin oaks a few miles to the west. I compared the poem's description of how to get to this lagoon with my own drawings. As soon as I finished mapping a path, I'd set out—alone. If there was a hidden source of power in Corona and I found it, I'd have the leverage I needed to get into the guard. Forget about the Winged Beast and the maps—I'd be undeniable. After staying up most of the night, I charted what I thought was a likely route. Then I folded it in my pocket and set out before dawn. A night of princess-sitting hadn't turned out to be such a royal waste of time after all.

The air was crisp, like a fresh piece of paper, and I felt alert despite my lack of sleep. My blood was warm as it galloped through my veins. There was nothing I loved more than being out on an adventure. Best of all, the twin oaks were in a rural part of Corona that the guards weren't focused on at all. I saw a few red foxes, watchful and curious. My breath puffed white as I studied my compass and headed west. I must have walked for at least an hour, pausing only to drink from a brook. A few times I thought I heard some rustling behind me, but I kept going. At last I found the pair of oak trees, surrounded by berry bushes as described in the poem.

Berries shine in dew like rubies, outstretched arms guide seekers west.

I followed the trees' roots and found a boulder.

I scaled the boulder and discovered a path behind it. It was overgrown and barely visible, but with my compass, I found enough markers to assure me I was on to something. Then the path divided into three junctures.

Three divisions bring three decisions; remember, hearts know best.

I repeated the line in my head, realizing that "hearts know best" had to be a clue—it was too sappy even for a bad poet. The heart is on the left side of the body, so it had to be directing me that way. I decided to stay left.

At last the path became clearer. The grass was green as emeralds, just as the poem said. I followed it until I came to another boulder. I've always been a good climber, so the steep incline didn't scare me, though it was more difficult than I'd imagined. It was going to be harder to get down. I was glad I'd brought a rope. I could hitch it to the ledge and then use that to get down.

At the top, the boulder unexpectedly split, creating two walls with water running in between them. There'd been no mention of this in the poem. It was impossible to tell how deep the water was, and a ripple of fear went through me.

Ergh! I growled with frustration as sweat stung my eyes.

Don't be a wimp, I told myself as my arms and legs shook. *Pretend you don't feel it.*

I could see that on the other side of the gulch the walls connected again, and I would be able to walk to the lagoon, which I imagined was even bluer than the water that flowed beneath me. The rocks were too far apart for me to walk with a leg on either side, but if I stretched my body across the gap, I could hold on to one side with my hands, bracing my feet on the other side. It was my only option, and I had come so far. I wasn't going to turn back without at least trying.

I put my hands on one ledge and placed my feet on the other side, and I began to traverse the gulch. Below me, water rushed over rocks. My arms began to tremble and my legs ached. I froze. A lump began to rise in my throat.

"Slide down."

Was that . . . *Rapunzel's* voice? No, no, no! Just when I thought things couldn't get any worse, they did. I glanced up. Rapunzel was there—standing at the top of the boulder.

"What are you doing here?" I asked, squeezing my eyes shut. If I couldn't see the water, maybe I could overcome this stupid fear.

"Looking for the lagoon with you! Don't you see? This is exactly the kind of thing I was hoping would happen when you became my lady-in-waiting," she said. I gnashed my teeth, my arms shaking with fatigue as she joined me, assuming the same position. Her proximity made me sweat even more.

"This is so uncomfortable!" Rapunzel said, turning to face me with an improbable and unwelcome grin. "I'm going down there. It'll be so much easier to walk through the water than scale this ravine! Come on!"

"You first," I said. My left hand slipped and I almost cried out.

"Okay!" she said. I heard a splash. "Wow, that's chilly! And yeah, we can walk. It's only waist-deep. Come on, I'll catch you."

Only waist-deep, I told myself as my cramping feet began to pulse with pain. I had no choice. I closed my eyes and let go.

9
RAPUNZEL

I caught Cassandra and helped steady her on her feet.

"You were pretty scared up there, huh?" I said. Her straight line of a mouth let me know she was mad that I'd followed her, but her eyes were wide and vulnerable.

"Not at all," she said, refusing to meet my gaze.

"So I was right!" I said, walking through the cold, clear water. "You thought the lagoon was a real place, too. I knew it! And those *were* maps in your room, weren't they?"

"Yes . . ." Cassandra said, walking behind me. "I

just wanted to make sure it was safe before you came here with me."

"I appreciate that, but what you need to know about me is that I love adventure. I was in a tower for eighteen years, so I really want to see the world," I said.

"You should go home," she said. "Now."

"No way," I said. "I feel more at home exploring the kingdom than learning etiquette!"

"Doesn't matter," she said. "It's not safe."

"But it's fun," I said.

"Does anyone know where you are?" Cassandra asked. Her eyes narrowed. "Did you tell Eugene?"

"No." I hadn't seen Eugene since the night before. After Cassandra left my room, I sent Pascal to follow her. I instructed him to come get me if she went anywhere. "Why can't we let anyone know, though?"

"About the ancient secret power of the kingdom?" she asked.

"Yes," I said. "Why shouldn't my family know about it?"

"If this information got in the wrong hands, there could be real trouble."

"What kind of trouble? I want to know. I *need*

to know," I said. And then I saw it. *We* saw it. We gasped. "Whoa! It's the lost lagoon!"

A lone bird sang an elaborate tune.

"It's so . . . blue," Cassandra said.

The sun was shining on the water in a dazzling display of light. A school of yellow fish slid beneath the surface, sun dancing on their fins. In another corner, bright orange starfish clung to rocks. The walls surrounding the lagoon were covered in bright green moss.

"Have you ever seen someplace so . . . beautiful?" I asked. Cassandra shook her head. The crystal blue beckoned me. "I can't take it," I said, unable to contain my awe. "I'm diving in!" I stripped down to my camisole and bloomers and leapt in, allowing myself to sink before I swam back toward the light. The cool, clear water encircled me like an embrace. "Cassandra, you have to come in!"

"I can't," she said.

"Yes you can!" I said. "Just jump."

"No," she said, her brow furrowed.

"Why not?" I asked. I ducked under the water, gulped a mouthful, and resurfaced as a fountain.

"Because," she said, crossing her arms.

"Because what?" I asked.

"Ugh!" she grunted. "Where is this secret power?"

"It's in here somewhere," I said. This wasn't just water. It was like water from a dream: cool, soft, and sweet. I turned a somersault, blew bubbles, and kicked a splashy invitation. I bobbed back up. "It feels so good! It isn't even that cold—"

"You think I care about being cold?" she snapped. She turned away.

I paused, treading water. "Cassandra?"

"You don't get it, Rapunzel," she said, throwing her arms in the air. "I can't swim!"

10

CASSANDRA

"I can't swim!" I said.

Our kingdom was surrounded by water. There were 315 miles of ocean beach, 212 lakes, 121 ponds, 68 rivers, and 17 estuaries. And I couldn't swim. Why? Because of fear. Stupid fear.

I hated admitting this to Rapunzel. A fear of water was ridiculous in Corona. Who was I kidding? This stupid phobia would keep me out of the guard. But the words had tumbled out of my mouth before I had a chance to stop them.

"Then I need to teach you," she said, beaming up at me.

"Huh?" I asked. Why wasn't she laughing at me?

Who in their right mind wouldn't think I was a total idiot for being a Coronan who didn't know how to swim? "I don't get it."

"I'll teach you how to swim," she said, as though this were no big deal—as though I wouldn't be the laughingstock of the guard if my secret got out. She just swam in place and spoke in a plain, honest voice. "I understand why it's scary, but I think you're going to love it. You *do* know that I just learned to *sit*, right?"

I stifled a grin.

She ducked underwater and then resurfaced with her hair stuck to the front of her face. "How do I look?"

"Like a wet dog," I said, and she shook out her hair like a playful puppy.

"Can you imagine what that would have looked like before I cut my hair?" She laughed and pushed her hair aside. "Come on, it's shallow over there."

She did another somersault and then swam to a ledge with steps leading down to the water. I walked around the edge until I got to the rock steps.

"It's perfect. You just need to come over and put your feet in. That's the first step." I climbed down the ledge and was about to stick a foot in when

CHAPTER TEN

Rapunzel said, "Oh, and it's easier if you take off your boots."

"Have you ever taught anyone how to swim before?" I asked her as I pulled off my boots.

"Nope. You're my first student." She grinned. "I don't know if security briefed you, but I've been living in a tower for eighteen years."

"So why should I trust you?" I asked, dipping my bare toes into the water.

"Why shouldn't you?" she said, looking genuinely confused. "Have I done something to make you not trust me?"

"No," I said. It was the truth. She smiled up at me, aglow in the bright sunshine. "How did *you* learn how to swim?"

"It's amazing how fast you can pick something up when your life depends on it. But I've taught myself a lot of stuff, and I've always said that the first step is the hardest."

I closed my eyes and took a breath, and then I opened them and dipped my toes into the water. She was right. The water was perfect.

"Good," she said. "Now take another step forward." I did. The water came up to my knees.

"This seems like a good enough start for today, doesn't it?" I said. "I'm done."

"No way," she said. "We've barely started. So what I do when I'm scared is I think about my favorite recipe. I go through it step by step in as much detail as possible."

"I don't bake," I said.

"I know," she said. "But maybe you could think about your favorite . . . I don't know . . . thing to throw? It has to be a procedure of some kind."

"Okay. I can tell you about the way to polish your armor," I said.

"Okay," she said. "Sounds good. Each time you tell me a step, take a step forward."

"First you hang your suit of armor up to make sure every piece is properly aligned," I said, "and that there's no rust."

"Step forward," she said.

I took a deep breath and did so. I was up to my thighs now.

"Then you attach the foot coverings," I said. "After inspecting them, of course."

"That makes sense," she said. "Step forward."

The water seeped up to my waist, and I kept thinking about my suit of armor—or the one I longed to have when I became a guard, anyway.

"Then you need to polish the chest plate. With a soft cloth, work in circles, going outward."

"That sounds like a step," Rapunzel said. I ventured out farther, still picturing the armor in my mind. "What's next?"

I closed my eyes. "Then you work on the arms. The arms can be tricky because of the joints."

"Look where you are," Rapunzel said.

"I don't need to," I said, fearing that I would lose my courage if I opened my eyes. "I can feel that I'm up to my neck."

"But I want you to watch my arms," she said. I opened my eyes. "You're going to move them back and forth like this as you tell me about the next step in preparing armor for battle."

I followed her lead with my arms and told her about polishing the helmet, making sure to include the details about the mouth cover.

"All right," she said. "You're almost there. Next you just move your legs as if you're running."

I opened my mouth to speak but she stopped me, saying, "Cassandra, I'm right in front of you, and that rock is right behind you. You're an arm's length away from safety. So why don't you tell me about the next step, after polishing the helmet. And then take your final step away from the rocks."

"The legs," I said, stepping into the open water while pushing my hands back and forth. "You have to get the thigh plates and the shins. For those, you want to make up-and-down—whoa! I'm doing it!" I said. Rapunzel laughed. "I'm doing it! I'm doing it!" Then I suddenly forgot what to do with my arms and they stopped working. My head went under, but before I could even shut my eyes, Rapunzel had swept me up and pulled me to the safety of the rock.

"You did it!" she said.

"I went swimming!" I said.

"You're welcome," she said, even though I hadn't thanked her. "That was just treading water. The next time we'll practice swimming. I really can't believe that you didn't know how. You're the bravest person I've ever met."

"What are you talking about?" I asked. Knowing how to swim in a seaside kingdom wasn't heroic. It was basic.

"You just faced your fear," she said. I waved her off. She held my gaze. "Why are you scared of water?"

"It's nothing."

"Facing your biggest fear is *nothing*?" she asked. "You should be really proud."

"That and a coin will get me a cup of coffee," I said.

CHAPTER TEN

"It will?" Rapunzel asked.

"It's a phrase," I said, taking in her puzzled expression. "An idiom, you know?"

"I don't," Rapunzel said, squinting into the early morning sun. "Actually, there's so much I don't know, sometimes it makes me dizzy."

"When I was six I almost drowned," I said. Her honesty had caught me off guard, and I just started talking.

"That must have been terrifying," Rapunzel said. "No wonder you're scared of the water."

"I'm alive." I shrugged. "So who cares?"

"Me," she said. "Tell me what happened. I mean, if you want to."

"It's in the past," I said. For reasons I didn't understand, I *did* want to tell her, but I didn't trust that the lump in my throat wouldn't rise again.

"It's your story," Rapunzel said. "That makes it important."

The memory hovered in my throat. We sat in silence for a few moments, staring at the water. Patches of shadows on the lagoon darkened and lightened. A breeze rustled the leaves. Birds warbled back and forth in conversation. I took a breath, and before I knew it, the story came out.

"I was at the seashore with my father. He told

me a hundred times to stay close to him, but I saw a crab I wanted to catch. I followed it. A wave snatched me up and carried me out. My father saved me. He was so mad. I was scared twice that day. Once by the water and once by my father's anger. I've never been able to get in the water since."

"But you did today," she said.

"Yeah."

She hadn't laughed. She hadn't judged.

As the sun climbed over a hill, the patches of shade dissolved. Right in front of us, beneath the surface, was a shining light so bright I had to squint. A cluster of tiny stones was lit up like blue flames—or were they jewels? Was this the ancient power? Rapunzel gripped my hand. This time I didn't flinch.

11
RAPUNZEL

"Here," I said as soon as I swam back up to the surface with one of the blue gems. There were so many of them, and when I touched them underwater they were warm, as if they had captured the sun that had appeared to set them on fire. It had taken some effort to pull one away, and I squeezed it tightly as I returned to Cassandra. I held on to a ledge and passed the gem to her. She placed it in her palm, studying its texture and size and then holding it up to the sun.

"Is it possible that it's just glass?" Cassandra asked, turning it over again in her hand. Here on dry land, it didn't seem that it could be precious. It was pretty, but not extraordinary.

"How can that be?" I asked, pointing to the cluster of blue gems. "These have to be connected to the stones in the poem. Remember? 'Truth was sealed in precious stones—they hold the ancient power . . . that underlies Corona's strength and binds us like sun to flower.'"

"Yeah. Get another one," Cassandra said, all business. "Maybe this one's a dud."

"Okay," I said, taking a deep breath and diving back under. The lagoon was so pure and clear that it didn't hurt to open my eyes when I was underwater. I pried another blue gem away from the rock. Swimming back up, I felt the smile on my face and the joy in my limbs. I had a mission now; I had work to do in Corona—to find its ancient power! For the first time I felt like I had a purpose in my new home. "How is this one?"

"It also just seems like glass," Cassandra said with a shrug. She glanced up at the sun. Her face clouded with worry. "It's time to go back. It's after breakfast and you're missing."

"I left my mom a note telling her I'd gone for a stroll for some exercise," I said, pulling myself out of the water and sitting beside Cassandra on the rock.

"Smart," Cassandra said. I smiled, sensing her respect at my planning. "I'm sure that bought us this much time."

"We can't leave now," I said. "We've only scratched the surface of this mystery!"

"We'll have to come back," Cassandra said as she put her boots on.

We. I grinned. Even if we'd started out the day separately, we were in this together now. It was so much fun to have a friend who actually talked!

"As soon as possible," I said, squeezing water out of my hair.

"Without a doubt," Cassandra said as she tied her boots. "And until then, it's our secret."

"But maybe our families could help us figure this out," I said as I pulled my dress over my head.

"No," Cassandra said. "If the king or queen ever thought I put you in danger . . ."

"I would tell them it was my fault, that I followed you," I said.

"It doesn't matter," Cassandra said. "You don't get it. *I'll* be punished."

"I won't tell. And Eugene would never, either."

"You can't even tell Eugene," Cassandra said. "This place could be the key to protecting Corona forever. We need to figure this out before anyone else does. And I want to learn how to swim. This can be my new training ground. If I'm going to make it into the guard—"

She paled.

"The guard? But you're my lady-in-waiting," I said, watching her face closely. She let her silence speak for her until I realized. "Oh. You don't want to be."

"I was born to defend this kingdom," she said.

I recognized the look in her eyes.

"Then I'll help you," I said, because I knew what it felt like to have a dream burning inside, like a candle on a moonless night. Being a princess was going to take a lot of lessons. But being a friend was something I could do right away. "I won't tell anyone. You need to train. I can help you."

"Actually . . . there *is* one move I really need to learn. No one has been able to do it for a hundred years—and if I could do it, I'd be guaranteed a place in the guard."

"What is it?" I asked.

CHAPTER ELEVEN

"It's called the Winged Beast. It takes two people to do it," Cassandra said. "But it's dangerous—as in life-threateningly dangerous."

"I'll help you," I said firmly.

"Are you sure?" she asked.

"Definitely."

"Okay," Cassandra said. She nodded, smiling for the first time since I'd spotted her in the field from far away. "But now I have to teach you which fork to eat your waffles with and stuff. Come on. Let's go, Raps."

"Raps," I repeated. I liked it. It was short and to the point, like my new hair. Best of all, it had come from Cassandra.

"You got it, Cass," I said.

And we bid goodbye to our lagoon.

For now.

Later that night, I made bracelets out of the gems. Using a hot needle, I burned a hole through the center and threaded it with a thin strip of leather. I gave Cass hers after dinner.

"What's this?" she asked.

"A bracelet," I said. I showed her mine. "See? I have one, too."

"Matching bracelets? I appreciate it, but jewelry isn't really my thing."

"Like poetry and cookies?" I asked.

She just smiled and shook her head.

Later, however, when she was preparing me for a luncheon with my parents, I saw it was tied around her wrist in a very complicated knot.

INTERLUDE

RAPUNZEL: *For a while, Cass and I went to the lagoon every day, the book of poetry in hand, to solve the mystery of the poem. Cass became a good swimmer, but we hadn't found any clues about the ancient power of the lagoon beyond the gems that sparkled in the sunlight.*

CASSANDRA: *Soon it turned bitterly cold and terrible storms kept us from visiting the lagoon. "When the storms pass, we'll get back to solving this," I told Raps. I had plans for myself in Corona.*

RAPUNZEL: *While the weather raged, my days indoors were filled with preparations for my coronation, along with lessons in diplomacy, geography, and economics. The closer we got to the big event, the more public appearances there were. Each obligation had rules, dresses, shoes, and hairstyles that went with it. I missed the days of the lagoon—the freedom and sunshine.*

CASSANDRA: *I hated coronation preparation. I itched to get out and do something. If I had to fasten one more bustle or dust one more layer of face powder on Raps or myself I was going to bust. I needed to GET OUT.*

RAPUNZEL: *Right before the coronation, in a moment I didn't see coming, Eugene proposed to me. As in, proposed marriage! In front of a crowd! I panicked. Even though I love Eugene with all my heart, I couldn't say yes. I was just not ready to be a wife!*

CASSANDRA: *On the night Eugene proposed, Raps was paler than a fish's underbelly.*
"Come on," I said. "Let's get out of here and have some fun."

RAPUNZEL: *Cass led me through a secret tunnel, and we escaped the walls of the kingdom. We rode like the wind through forests and clearings, caught lightning bugs in our hands, and spun cartwheels on the beach. We paddled across rivers and leapt through tide pools. I felt like I could do anything, be anything!*

CASSANDRA: *The night was ours. I decided to show Raps the weird spikey rocks on the other side of a stony bridge.*

"These rocks are in the same place where they found the miracle that saved your mother and you," I told her. The air seemed to thicken and hum where we stood.

Raps reached out and touched one of the rocks—and that's when the energy around us turned dark and dangerous.

Something was happening. I didn't understand, but it had to do with Raps and those rocks. It was as if they recognized her.

"Run!" I said, fear spinning my blood. "Run!"

RAPUNZEL: *As we raced over the crumbling bridge, my hair began to grow. And grow. And grow. It was scary. Relentless, even. More spikey rocks sprang out of the earth as though they were chasing us. The roots* *of my scalp stung as we ran back to the kingdom and my hair unfurled behind me. The mouth of danger was snapping at our heels. We survived the journey back to the castle. Barely.*

CASSANDRA: *We returned to the castle at daybreak and spent all morning trying to cut Raps's insanely long—and now blond—hair a million different ways, but it wouldn't break.*

RAPUNZEL: *After several hours, I accepted that my hair was back and that I couldn't cut it. I couldn't conceal it. I couldn't escape it. My past had returned to me, and my neck ached under the weight of it.*

"Don't tell anyone what happened," Cass begged.

"Why can't I tell the truth?" I asked. "We need all the help we can get."

"If anyone finds out what happened, I'll probably be sent to a convent. Forever."

I nodded.

"Do you promise?" she asked, locking her eyes with mine. There was terror behind them.

Then Eugene knocked on the door.

"Not even him," Cass warned.

INTERLUDE

CASSANDRA: *We couldn't hide her hair for long. And once it was revealed, I lived in fear. If Raps told anyone I was the one who led her outside the kingdom, I didn't know what my punishment would be, but I knew I could forget being captain of the guard someday. I could forget my destiny. I could forget being me.*

RAPUNZEL: *I told my parents that I acted alone. They believed me—though my father forbade me to leave the walls of the kingdom again. As for Eugene, I told him I'd just woken up with my hair like this. But he knew I was hiding something, and it was killing him. It was killing me, too! After all, things had been really weird between us after I hadn't accepted his marriage proposal. I couldn't stand the distance between us, so I broke down and told him the truth about how my hair had grown back. Eugene and I finally felt like us again.*

"I'm sorry I kept a secret from you," I said, embracing him. "From now on, no more secrets."

"What about Cassandra?" he asked.

"That's between her and me," I said, and I took a deep breath.

I finally felt better. At least, most of the time. . . .

PART TWO

12

RAPUNZEL

"Is this grass even greener than before?" I asked Cass as we made our way down the emerald path to the lagoon for the first time in six months. It had only been a few days since I'd told Eugene the truth about my hair, and it had been haunting me until now. The warm spring breeze wiped away my guilt as it fluttered the leaves above us. I couldn't stop smiling. The stormy season had been long and cold, but today felt like summer—at least in the sun. I stopped and picked a blade of grass. "It's a brighter shade, closer to parakeet than emerald."

"Parakeet?" Cass asked, her maps and drafting

tools under her arm. "Green is green, Raps." She gestured for me to keep walking. "Come on, we can't spend all morning looking at the grass—we have to make the most of our time at the lagoon. The Hervanian royalty are arriving tonight for their long stay, and the Hidden Moon Festival is coming up. Your schedule is going to start getting crazy again."

"Will you tell me what the festival is all about again?" I asked, tucking the blade of grass into my pocket and hurrying to catch up with her. I couldn't believe there was another big event coming up so quickly. The coronation had only just happened.

"It's usually called the Flower Moon Festival because it's in April—" Cass said.

"And that's when all the flowers begin to bloom!" I said, noticing a patch of purple snapdragons at the base of the boulder.

"Yeah, I guess people are into that kind of thing," Cass said as we climbed. "So, every year, on the first full moon in April, all the villagers come to the castle to show off their skills and to learn from others, and there's a performance, and a big ball, of course. This year is going to be bigger than ever because it's a hidden moon, hence the change of name. . . ."

CHAPTER TWELVE

"An eclipse," I said.

"Exactly," Cass said. "Some people think that's good luck; others think it's bad."

"What do you think?" I asked as we lowered ourselves into the gulch. The water was colder than I remembered.

"I'm not superstitious," Cass said, leading the way. "All I know is that you and I are going to be *very* busy. The queen has put us in charge of a lot. We'll be kicking off the festivities by showing off one of your talents."

"Like painting?" I asked.

"Don't take this personally, but it's not too exciting to watch someone paint, especially for a crowd. I was thinking more like fencing," she said.

"Sure, that'd be fun. . . ."

"And then I'll have to lead a few activities, while you'll be expected to make appearances all over the festival. Show your face, shake some hands, kiss some babies. You get the idea."

"Wow," I said as the lagoon came into sight. I'd forgotten how beautiful it was! The water was a deep turquoise, and the sun glinted off the surface like tiny sparks. I sat on the mossy bank and leaned over to test the water with my hand.

"I'm going to explore over there," Cass said,

pointing toward the opposite side of the lagoon. "That's where I need to fill in the missing places on my maps."

"Okay," I said, staring at my reflection on the surface. My eyes grew wide. The sight of my hair still surprised me. I dipped my toes in the water. It was chilly but wonderful, and I couldn't help thinking of the time I'd spent there with Cass, teaching her how to swim. My stomach tightened, as it did so often these days when I thought about how angry Cass would be if she knew I'd told Eugene the truth about our night out. I just needed to convince her that she could trust Eugene. Then she'd understand and everything would be okay. I wondered if it was too cold to wade as I hiked up my dress and sank in to my calves. Yes! It was. But the water was no less beautiful for its temperature.

"This has to be something important," Cass called, bringing my attention back to the moment as she looked out from behind the waterfall.

"What?" I asked, rushing over to her.

"Check it out," Cass said. What had been a gushing waterfall a few months ago was now just a faint trickle.

"What happened to the waterfall?" I asked.

"The storms were so wild. Maybe the landscape

shifted and redirected the water. But Raps," she said, pointing. "Look what was hiding behind it."

Without the solid wall of water falling from above, there was a good view of the space underneath the waterfall. There was a semicircle of smooth, flat rocks, forming a table of sorts.

"It looks like it was built by people," I said, stepping into the chilly water.

"What is it, though?" Cass said.

"A historian could answer that," I said excitedly. If this was a clue, we'd be one step closer to solving the mystery of the lagoon's ancient power. And that seemed more important now than ever—something I could do that would help the kingdom and not disappoint my parents or hurt my best friend.

"We need to see Xavier," Cass said. "He's the only one who might have the information that will help us put this all together. You'll finally get that history lesson you've been wanting."

13
CASSANDRA

Getting Raps through the market to Xavier's shop wasn't easy. She was so easily distracted by the shops and vendors. To be honest, I loved the market, too, but we were on a mission, after all.

"Oh, Cass, do you smell that?" she asked as we walked by the baker's shop.

I did smell something delicious, but I had to keep us on track.

"Priorities!" I said, guiding her onward, even though my mouth watered and my stomach growled as the scent of baked goods wafted toward us.

"And look! There's a paint seller," she said, pointing to a girl about our age with curly red hair tied back in a ponytail. "If I knew that there was someone in town selling art supplies, I'd visit the market more often!"

"We have such a busy day," I said, trying to keep her on task. "We don't have time to go shopping."

"One second." She skidded to a halt. "Are you suggesting we *don't* buy some of those pastries?"

"Raps, if the princess visits the bakery, the baker is going to want to have her whole family greet you, and it would be rude if you didn't oblige her—"

"It'll only take a second if *you* go and buy them," I said. "I'll wait here."

"Okay," I said, more quickly than I cared to admit. "Fine—but put your cloak on. We don't have time for a fan club meeting!"

"The smell got to you, didn't it?" she asked.

"Be right back."

I went inside to buy the pastries. When I returned, Raps was chatting with the paint seller, despite her promise to stay put.

"Excuse me," I said to the paint seller, taking Raps by the arm. "We're in a rush."

"Oh, but we were—" the girl started, but I gave her a curt smile and hurried Raps along.

"Bye, Dahlia," Raps said, waving to her over her shoulder.

I unwrapped the pastries as we walked and handed one to Raps.

"She's nice," Raps said. "And she's a professional artist. Maybe she could teach art at the festival."

"The official castle portrait painter does that already. Come on, let's eat and walk," I said. I couldn't help it. I devoured the pastry. It was delicious, warm, and sticky with half-melted sugar, and topped with blackberries and cream. "This is pretty good."

"Good? More like the best thing I've ever eaten!" Raps said, wiping her hands on her hanky.

"Raps, your middle name is hyperbole," I said.

"What can I say? I like a lot of things!"

"And we're here," I said, gesturing to the entrance of Xavier's shop.

The shop was small and dark but as neat and organized as my weapons closet. Hammers, anvils, chisels, and nails hung on one wall. Horseshoes, keys, and locks hung on another. Raps and I pulled up a pair of stools while Xavier stoked the furnace.

"Princess, it is such a great honor to meet you.

I'm so glad you've come to my shop," Xavier said with a bow.

"It's I who am honored to meet you," Rapunzel said with a curtsy. "I know I have so much to learn about Corona and that you are the man to help."

"You flatter me," Xavier said. "But I'll do my best. Now, if you can wait just a moment, I'll be right with you ladies. I must get the morning fire stoked for the day's work."

"Are those the new style of daggers I've been hearing about?" I asked, admiring weapons on a nearby table.

"Indeed," Xavier said. "The king has ordered them for the guard. They're the most dangerous daggers I've seen."

"In what way?" I asked.

"Feel this," he said as he handed a dagger to me. It was so light. I ran my finger along the thin blade. My pulse quickened with excitement. Six months had been a long time to think about nothing but princess stuff. "It can cut through armor as though it were paper. It would be terrible if one got into the wrong hands."

Danger had been on my mind lately. Ever since Raps's hair had grown back, I'd been living with a marble of fear that bobbed back and forth between my stomach and throat.

Yes, we'd gone on adventures before, but this one had rocked the kingdom.

The king and queen were trying to believe that she had acted alone that night, but they were uneasy. They sensed there was a missing piece. The thought of going to a convent—or whatever punishment they might come up with—kept me up at night. And what was worse was the thought that I would never be a part of the Coronan guard. Every time this thought passed through my mind, I broke out in a cold sweat. What I needed more than ever was to take control of my future, to show that I was a Coronan through and through. I needed to discover the ancient power of Corona. I needed to solve the mystery of the lagoon. That would grant me freedom.

Xavier sat down with us. I handed the dagger back, handle first, in the manner of a trained soldier.

"So," Xavier said, rubbing his hands together. "How may I be of service?"

"Well, I have many questions about the history of Corona . . ." Rapunzel started.

"What do you think this is?" I asked, cutting to

the chase and handing him Raps's sketch of the semicircle of stones.

Xavier cleared his throat and studied it for a moment. "Looks like an ancient Saporian ceremony circle. Where did you find this?"

"On the outskirts of the village," I said, before Raps could respond. She was too honest for her own good sometimes.

"The one by the community stables?" Xavier asked.

"Yes," I said.

"What kind of ceremonies took place at these circles?" Raps asked.

"All kinds!" Xavier said. "Birth celebrations, death rituals, weddings, harvest prayers, you name it. I can direct you to more of them if you like. They are beautiful, aren't they? That's some first-class stone masonry. Is there anything else I can help you with?"

"Actually, yes. We want to know more about this poem," Raps said, pushing the book across the table to him.

"Oh, my. What do we have here?" Xavier asked, the corners of his eyes crinkling with a smile as he read over the poem. "An actual physical copy of 'The Lost Lagoon'?"

"You know it?" she asked.

"Of course," he said, the smile spreading across his face. "Though a printed edition . . . Why, this is rare indeed." His large hands delicately turned the pages of the book. "Where did you find this?"

"In the library," Raps said.

"Libraries hold great treasures, and this is a true gem," Xavier said. Raps and I exchanged a quick smile.

"What do you know about this poem?" I asked.

" 'The Lost Lagoon' is one of the oldest poems in Corona. It's a legend that's been handed down by word of mouth alone—at least that's what I thought. Turns out it's been written down, as well. Fascinating."

"Legend?" I asked. "So, you're sure no place like this exists?"

"This is just a poet's fancy. A long time ago, before even I was born, people searched high and low for this place. They could never find it—even those cartographers who made their life's mission to chart every inch of this kingdom."

"Really?" I asked. It was pretty hard not to smile, knowing I'd outsmarted a bunch of old cartographers.

"Really," Xavier said, and he held up the book.

CHAPTER THIRTEEN

"What you have here is just a story. But it intrigued you, so that means it's a good one. People think it's easy to write a romance, but it's not true. Only the great love stories last."

"A romance?" Raps said. "Tell me more!"

"I thought the poem is about Corona's greatest power," I said. "Not love."

"It's about both," Xavier said, and stroked his chin. "You know the story of Herz Der Sonne and General Shampanier, right?"

"No," Raps said.

"Surely you know it, Cass," Xavier said. "We commemorate it every year when we celebrate the Day of Hearts."

"I've heard the story, but I never really paid attention to the details," I said. Xavier raised his eyebrows in surprise. "What? I'm not really a hearts kind of girl." I gestured to Raps. "She'll eat it up."

"Yes, tell me!" Raps said.

"More than two hundred years ago, the king of Corona, Herz Der Sonne, created a system of tunnels to move knights and supplies around the kingdom," Xavier said. "We were at war with Saporia, after all, and these tunnels gave us a strategic advantage."

"I've heard of them . . ." Raps said, glancing at me uneasily. The tunnels had played a crucial role in getting Rapunzel out of the kingdom the night her hair had grown back.

"He had kept detailed maps of these tunnels in a book," Xavier said. "And General Shampanier, the ruler of Saporia, stole it. She was a serious warrior, and was going to use the tunnels to attack Corona. She probably would have conquered us—but at the end of the book she discovered Herz Der Sonne's love confession. He was head over heels for this strong, intelligent woman."

"Really?" Raps said. Xavier nodded. "That's so romantic!"

"What does this have to do with the lagoon?" I asked.

"This poem was written during the Era of Unity, when Herz Der Sonne and General Shampanier married and joined the countries together to create Corona as we know it," Xavier said. "There was an explosion of romantic poetry—and 'The Lost Lagoon' was one that really captured the people's imagination."

"Are you sure there isn't a military tale in there, as well?" I asked. "We're talking about the greatest power in Corona, right? That can't be cuddling."

CHAPTER THIRTEEN

"Cass!" Raps laughed.

"I'm no scribe, but of course it takes place during a conflict," Xavier said. "Otherwise where would the drama be?"

"Xavier," said a man who emerged from the back room. He had dark hair and piercing blue eyes and was so tall that he had to stoop to clear the door-frame. He was holding one of the new daggers. "I believe we can make this dagger even more deadly by adjusting the radius of the—" He looked up, noticing us for the first time. "Hello, there."

"This is my new assistant, Marco. He's a man of many talents," Xavier said.

"Thank you," Marco said, and he smiled enthusiastically.

"Marco, this is the princess Rapunzel and her lady-in-waiting, Cassandra."

"I'm honored," Marco said with a bow. Raps smiled and nodded in response. "I've heard so many wonderful things about you, Princess. To what do we owe the distinction of this visit?"

"These young ladies have discovered an actual copy of the old poem 'The Lost Lagoon,'" Xavier said.

"That's remarkable," Marco said, focusing on the slim green book.

"Isn't it?" Xavier said. "They've found a treasure in the royal library."

"One of the few copies of the poem. Yes, of course," Marco said. "I just knew amazing things would happen if I came to work for you, Xavier. And here's the perfect example. The legend about the ancient power of Corona has always been one of my favorites."

"So you believe it's about more than love?" I asked Marco.

"Absolutely," Marco said.

"Do you think it's real?" Raps asked.

"Unfortunately, no. But it's nice to dream, isn't it?" said Marco. "I'm a bit of a dreamer myself."

"I have to agree," Xavier said as Marco returned to the back room. "Fanciful imaginings help us lose ourselves, and we all need to be a little bit lost sometimes, don't we? It's how we find our way."

"That's really true," Rapunzel said with a look of wonder.

"So you're one hundred percent sure there's nothing real about this—no ancient power to be discovered?" I asked. I was not about to let this turn to a discussion about dreams.

"Yes," Xavier said.

CHAPTER THIRTEEN

"We need to get going," I said, glancing at the sun lowering outside of Xavier's window.

"We do?" Raps asked.

"You have a dance lesson, remember?" I said. "If I don't have you dressed, shoed, and ready to allemande in thirty minutes, Monsieur LaFleur will have me pirouette right off a cliff."

"He's a good teacher," Rapunzel said, though I could tell she was trying not to laugh. "Just a very punctual man."

"Come on, Raps," I said, nodding toward the door. "Let's go."

As I straightened her dress before her dance class, Rapunzel said, "I wish you'd just let me tell Eugene the whole truth about the night my hair grew back."

"No way," I told her.

"I wish you would understand what kind of person Eugene is," Rapunzel said. "I trust him with my life."

"Right—*your* life. This is mine. And I'm not getting banished if I can help it."

"Hello, girls," Queen Arianna said, releasing a shot of adrenaline into my veins. Gosh, she walked quietly. I guess practicing graceful movements *did* pay off. My palms, suddenly slippery, fumbled with the buttons of Raps's dress. Even more than the king, Queen Arianna seemed to sense that Raps's story didn't add up.

"Hi, Mom," Raps said.

"Hello," I said, focused on my task. "Rapunzel is ready for her dance class."

"Not a minute too soon," Queen Arianna said as the clock struck.

"Or a minute too late," Raps said with a smile, and dashed inside the ballroom.

I curtsied to the queen and hurried to Rapunzel's room to set out her gown for dinner, my heart beating in time to Monsieur LaFleur's metronome.

14

RAPUNZEL

"One and two and three and four and one and two and three and four," Monsieur LaFleur counted. He clapped the rhythm with his hands while I attempted to allemande with an imaginary partner. "Light on your feet, arms in a frame, and turn a rosette!"

I tripped over myself and Monsieur LaFleur signaled the musicians to stop. He clicked his tongue and shook his head.

"*Non, non, non.* This will never do. *Pas de tout!*" He drew in a deep breath through long, quaking nostrils. "Princess, in order for you to allemande, your mind as well as your body must be present.

The two must work in harmony, otherwise the dance is flawed."

"Yes, monsieur," I said, bowing my head. I couldn't get my mind off the fact that I'd told Eugene about my adventure with Cass. She didn't suspect a thing, and that made it worse. It had felt so right to finally tell Eugene the truth, but my guilt over Cass nagged at me. "I'm sorry. I have a lot on my mind."

"Body, mind, and soul must come unite in this opulent dance, this purest expression of elegance. Are you ready?"

"Um, I think so?" I said.

"Very well," he said, and the musicians began again. I had just started to demi-coupé and fouetté when Monsieur LaFleur said, "What about your curtsy? *Mon cherie*, curtsies cannot just be cast aside like old cabbages!"

"Oops," I said.

"We need Eugene," he said. "I should have known."

"We do?" I asked. I loved Eugene, but I wasn't sure why he needed to be at this specific dance lesson.

"Of course, you are in love! There is nothing

more distracting. One must simply surrender to amour."

"I think you're right," I said.

Though it wasn't thoughts of Eugene that were distracting me, he would definitely make this dance class more fun. Monsieur LaFleur went to find him, and I went over why I had done the right thing by telling him that Cass had been the one to take me outside the kingdom. *Our relationship depends on openness and trust. He's my partner in all things. The secret of the lagoon is between Cass and me. I would never betray her. But my hair is mine—and the way it grew back is one of the biggest things that's ever happened to me. It's my weight to bear. I can't keep it from him without putting a wall between us.*

When Eugene walked through the door with that mischievous smile on his face, my heart shone.

"Get into position, my doves," Monsieur LaFleur said. The music began.

Eugene bowed and I curtsied. *He knows me,* I thought. In the midst of the chaos of having defied my parents and my hair growing back, it felt so good to be known. And I knew him, too. He wasn't going to tell a soul that Cass had been the one to take me out of the kingdom the night my hair grew back. Eugene could be trusted.

"I'm glad I told you," I whispered.

"Me too," he said. For a second, I rested my forehead on his chest.

"Ahem," Monsieur LaFleur said. "I know that dance is romantic, but we must resist breaking form. It is in the tension of desire and resistance that dance lives."

"This guy is quite a philosopher," Eugene muttered under his breath. I giggled, but I pulled my mouth straight when Monsieur LaFleur shot me a serious look. Eugene and I held each other's gaze as we danced the allemande across the ballroom. We were stepping in sync and moving on the beat. In fact, I could barely feel my feet touch the floor.

"Beautiful," Monsieur LaFleur said as we flew through the room, all the steps of the dance coming together with the music exactly as they were supposed to. "Charming!"

For a moment I felt like maybe, just maybe, everything was going to turn out okay.

15

CASSANDRA

"Where's the fire?" Eugene asked, seeming to appear out of nowhere. I was on my way to pick up Raps's new dress. His voice made me jump.

"Out of my way, Fitzherbert. I'm in a rush," I said, collecting myself. Raps was having dinner that night with Hervanian royalty, who were in Corona for an extended visit and to take part in the Hidden Moon Festival. Hervan, a small but feisty country, had at last made gestures of peace toward Corona, and the king and queen were eager to make their reconciliation official.

Queen Arianna had asked that Rapunzel wear

a gown made from blue silk that the marquis and the duchess had sent as a gift. Friedborg had been sewing it for months, and it was finally ready. "Not all of us spend our days getting massages," I continued. "Some of us have *work* to do."

I pushed past him and resumed my quick pace. I'd been avoiding him like a pox. He hadn't stopped pestering me about how Raps was doing since her hair had grown back. He was worried that she wasn't "sharing her feelings." Ugh. No matter how many times I told him that I had no idea what was going on, he wouldn't leave me alone about it. Just yesterday he'd said, "I can tell you know something."

"Not a thing," I'd replied. An easy smile had spread across his lips, but I wasn't having it. "Oh, don't try that stuff on me!"

"Cassandra," he said just as I was about to round the corner to the queen's chambers.

"I'm working, Eugene—" I began again.

"I know, I know, you're busy," he said, leaning against the wall.

"What is it?" I asked with a sigh. "Because I've already told you, I know nothing about the hair. . . ."

"Cassandra, Cassandra. Just relax, will you? For a second, maybe? I just wanted to let you know that

I'm hoping we can be friends. Whatever I've done to make you so annoyed with me, I apologize. Can't we start fresh?"

"I see what you're doing, Fitzherbert. You're trying to get me calm and off guard, hoping I'll crack. But there's nothing to crack! I know nothing. So just forget about it. Go work your 'smolder' on someone else."

"Actually, that's not what I'm doing," he said.

"Please," I said. Eugene was always trying to get something. "You're not trying to squeeze me for information?" I examined his face for any indication of lying, like twitching lips or rapidly blinking eyes.

"No," he said, as though he didn't have a worry in the world. As though he knew exactly what had happened.

I felt my blood drain to my feet.

He knew.

"She told you." I spoke so quietly I was barely audible. Surprise and fear flashed across his face.

"No!" he said, lying through his teeth. Ah, yes. Here was the Eugene I knew. He stammered. "Ra-Rapunzel? Tell me something about you? Never! That's the farthest thing from the truth. Rapunzel didn't say a word about you and that night."

My chest began to tighten as if pulled into a corset.

Reading faces to detect lies was part of a guard's training. His symptoms were classic: Tiny beads of sweat on his upper lip. Shifty eyes. Hiccups.

She'd told him. *She'd told him!*

"Cassandra, I really think you're (*hiccup*) jumping to conclusions."

"You're a terrible liar," I said.

"You're scary," Eugene said. "I mean, look (*hiccup*). We had a discussion about what happened. I won't (*hiccup*) say a word, I promise. I know you don't trust me, but you *can* trust me."

The air felt too thick to breathe. I strode to Friedborg's room, gathered the blue silk dress from her hands, and then ran back to my chambers to gather myself.

I immediately started to pack, throwing my belongings into a bag. I wasn't about to hang around here long enough for anyone to catch me. I'd leave in the night.

What was the point of staying in Corona? I couldn't trust my best friend. I couldn't go on even one little adventure without risking being sent to a convent. My chances of making it into the guard depended on finding an ancient power that had eluded us for so long it would probably take years to find.

What kind of life was this for me?

I opened my weapons closet and picked out the most essential items to bring with me.

Why would Rapunzel do this when she knew the consequences for me? The blue silk dress hung like a ghost of her.

"What were you thinking?" I asked the dangling dress. "You just *had* to tell your boyfriend? What about our friendship? Doesn't it mean anything to you?"

How could I have been so stupid as to trust her? And what else had she told him? Did he know about the lagoon? Had he known all this time about the swimming?

The tower struck five. She was done with her dancing lesson and her afternoon tea and was probably waiting for me back in her room. I needed to get her dressed and ready to meet the Hervanians. But the last thing I wanted to do was dress her. I wanted to open my maps and plan my route and get on my way to the life I was destined for, but she'd probably try to stop me.

Calm down, I told myself. I wouldn't let on that I knew. I'd just act normal and then leave in the night. *Be calm,* I repeated. *You are a soldier first, and a lady-in-waiting second.*

16

RAPUNZEL

After my dance lesson, the afternoon sun was warm and golden as I selected flowers for Cass to place in my braid. I was just about done when I saw a patch of red flowers, and I thought they would be striking against Cass's dark hair. She wasn't exactly a flower wearer, but maybe she'd let me pin one on her dress? The color would set off her fair skin so perfectly. And she could at least keep some in a vase by her bed. I refused to believe there was a person alive who didn't feel better with freshly cut flowers in her room.

I picked a few and headed back toward the

castle. The sharp grass prickled my toes and the slanted sunlight warmed my face and arms.

The dance with Eugene had erased my worries, or at least pushed them aside. Monsieur LaFleur was right—dancing was a tonic for the soul. There was something about moving in time to the music that had restored me, from my toes to my hair.

I smiled as I realized that, for the first time since I'd arrived at the castle, I was actually looking forward to a dinner with foreign nobility. Most of the time I was so aware of how out of place I was, how unfamiliar I was with the customs even after six months here, that I had to give myself a pep talk before each event. I had come to count on Cassandra's humor to get me through.

But tonight I actually felt prepared.

Cass had taught me the basics of Hervanian culture (they're brash but can be funny; distrustful but not mean-spirited) and I even knew to use that itty-bitty fork with the oysters—a Hervanian delicacy. When it came time to demonstrate the allemande, I was certain I'd please the visitors. And I couldn't deny it—I was looking forward to having Eugene's hand back on my waist, guiding me gently across the floor.

"Sunshine?"

CHAPTER SIXTEEN

I turned around to see Eugene squinting against the setting sun, his brow crinkled with worry.

"I was just thinking about you," I said, tucking a flower into his lapel.

"You were?" he asked.

"Want to walk me back to my room?" I asked. "I'm a little late, I think, and Cass has to make sure my dress fits. And we have to deal with this!" I smiled and pointed to my hair. "It's not so easy to tame this mane."

"I actually have to talk to you about something," Eugene said as we climbed the castle steps.

"My hair?" I asked. "You have more questions?"

"No," Eugene said. I noticed the lowering sun and I picked up the pace, heading down the long hallway toward my room. Eugene had to jog a little to keep up. "It's actually about Cassandra. You see, she's not in a great mood. I ran into her after our dance lesson and . . ."

"Eugene, how many times do I have to tell you? That's just Cass. She's not all bubbles and moonbeams. But it's just a mask. Inside she's a softy."

"Oh, yeah," Eugene said under his breath as we rounded the corner, approaching my door. "About as soft as a porcupine. Hey, can you slow down for a second?"

"Not really. I can't be late. I'm trying to embrace this princess thing. Ever since *that night*, I haven't exactly been in my parents' graces." I was slightly out of breath when we arrived at my door. I fiddled with the lock as I continued. "I promise, if you and Cass can just get to know each other, you'll see that on the inside she's the sweetest, kindest person, and deep down, as gentle as a—"

"How could you?" Cassandra asked, standing on the other side of the door with her hands balled up in fists. I could see the tension in her eyes, her neck, and her white knuckles.

". . . lamb?" I said, though my pounding heart told me that I was facing a lion.

"Cass, what's wrong? What happened?"

"I was trying to tell you," Eugene said.

"Leave us alone," Cass said to Eugene.

"Uh, Eugene?" I said, turning to him. "Can you give us a few minutes?"

"I'd really rather stay and explain in a calm, rational manner—" Eugene started.

"OUT!" Cass said, pointing at the door.

"I'll just be stepping out now," Eugene said. "Rapunzel. I promise, I didn't betray you."

I shut the door behind Eugene and turned to Cass. My heart pounded.

"Cass, whatever happened, it can't be that bad," I said.

"Not that bad, huh?" she said, her eyes hard. "You told him that I snuck you out of the kingdom? How could you?"

"Oh, um . . . that," I said.

"Yes, *that*! You told your boyfriend, the former thief—"

"He's more than just my boyfriend," I said. "And he's not a thief anymore."

"People don't change! You told *a criminal* a detail that puts my entire future at risk. I could be going to a convent, Rapunzel!" She didn't say my name; she spat it, and the sound of it hit me like dart. "And my lifelong dream of serving in the guard, for which I've been preparing for as long as I can remember? It's over. A convent is probably the best scenario, actually. I mean, I put the princess's life in danger. I'd never have any hope of being respected again."

"Cass, no! I would never let anyone speak ill of you. And you won't have to go anywhere," I said, rushing toward her. "Eugene won't say a word. I never would have told him if I thought he would."

"I can't take that risk," she said, handing me the blue silk dress I was supposed to wear that night.

The silk glistened. It had been sewn perfectly.

"What do you mean?" I asked. "Eugene and I are going to be king and queen one day. We can't have secrets. We just can't." Words were failing me. They were leaving my mouth, but they lost their meaning in the air between us.

There was a knock at the door.

"Rapunzel?"

"Mom?" I said. Wow. Her timing couldn't have been worse.

"Are you almost ready, dear? We'd like to greet our guests as a family. This is an important meeting."

"I just need a little more time," I said, feeling Cass fuming beside me. It was like standing next to a roaring fire. "I'll meet you in, say, ten minutes?"

"We don't have ten minutes, Rapunzel. I'll be right outside," Mom said.

I undressed and struggled into my new gown. Cassandra buttoned the back. Her fingers were cold against my skin.

"What do you mean you can't take that risk?" I whispered, wiping tears from my face.

"I'm leaving," she hissed. She fastened the final button, pulling the bodice tight. "You're ready now. It's time for you to go."

"I'm not going anywhere until you tell me what you mean," I whispered, turning around and gripping her shoulders.

"I'm going to find another castle, another kingdom. I can find work as a guard," she said, teeth gritted.

"Rapunzel?" Mom called from the other side of the door. "Timeliness is not only a respect we grant all castle guests, but the example we set. I will see you in the parlor in exactly two minutes." Her voice was gentle as always, but I could tell that she meant business.

"Okay!" I called. Then I held Cass by the shoulders. "You don't have to go."

"I do," she said. "And so do you."

Before I could stop her, she reached behind me and opened the door, sending me out to . . .

Monsieur LaFleur?

"Uh, can I help you?" I asked, totally taken aback by the sight of my dance teacher, who seemed to have appeared out of nowhere.

"What the . . . ?" Cassandra cocked an eyebrow. She looked just as surprised as I felt, which seemed to put a temporary pause on her fury. "Rapunzel is in a rush."

"I'm here to escort her," Monsieur said. He dabbed

his forehead with a handkerchief. "Dancers make the swiftest guides."

"Guiding her is my job," Cass said.

"Perhaps mademoiselle would like some last-minute pointers?" Monsieur LaFleur said, ignoring Cass and taking my arm.

"Thanks, but I think I've got it down now," I said as the three of us hurried down the long hallway. With Cass holding one arm and Monsieur LaFleur holding the other, I was hardly touching the ground.

"I've heard you possess an original transcript of one of my most favorite poems, 'The Lost Lagoon'?" Monsieur said.

"That's true," I said.

"What about it?" Cassandra asked. "And how did you hear about that?"

"Someone was inquiring in the library, and I couldn't help but overhear. . . ."

"Who?" Cass asked.

"An elegant cloaked person . . . Didn't hear a name. Princess, I just wanted to let you know that I am a student of all arts—poetry is the dance of words, is it not? And I would be most grateful if you would lend me your copy of that delectable poem. To see the original text would realize a life's dream of mine. . . ."

"That won't be happening anytime soon," Cass said.

"I'm not ready to part with it. It's just so special to me," I said as he bowed deeply and Cass ushered me into the parlor, where my mother, father, and Eugene were waiting.

"This doesn't mean I'm not leaving," Cass whispered.

"Okay," I said. "But, Cass, can you . . . ? For the safety of the kingdom . . ."

She paused, then nodded, knowing exactly what I meant.

17

CASSANDRA

Of course, I immediately returned to Rapunzel's room and secured the book. I locked it in my satchel, hurried to my chamber, and put it under the bed. Then I lit a candle and spread out my maps on the table in my room, trying to put it out of my mind that Monsieur LaFleur wanted that book. (*"The dance of words?"* *Who even talks like that?*)

As mad as I was at Rapunzel, something about the way his lip had been quivering gave me a terrible feeling. If it was true that someone was inquiring about the book at the library, then that was odd. If it was a lie, and Monsieur LaFleur had been somehow eavesdropping on us—that was worse.

Why am I worried about this book? I wondered. *I need to move on with my life!* I'd return the book to her as soon as the dinner was over—make it Raps's responsibility. Why should I stay here? I couldn't be in the guard. I couldn't even *train* for the guard because I was stuck in my dead-end princess-sitting job! We hadn't had time to try out the Winged Beast, despite our first conversation at the lagoon, because of all of Rapunzel's royal duties. I couldn't go on adventures without being threatened with a life of solitude and shame. Not to mention my fate was now in the hands of a massage-addicted dingbat!

Get back to your maps, Cassandra, I told myself. I took a deep breath and made some calculations. I could walk about twenty miles a day. It'd be better to walk toward the south, where the weather was warmer. If I couldn't find work for a while, the last thing I needed was to be out on the open road in the winter months. Just as I thought this, I heard a distant rumble of thunder.

Please, I thought. *Please no rain tonight.*

I refocused: the kingdoms were closer together in the south. That meant more danger, but also a greater need for soldiers. There would be rivers to cross no matter which direction I chose. At least I knew how to swim.

Because of Raps. *Raps. Ugh!*

The thought of her made me so mad! She said there couldn't be any secrets between Eugene and her. But why—especially when it meant sacrificing my future and everything I held dear? I'd read about romantic love in poems, and it seemed to me like a spell. Sounded great for the lovebirds, but what about the other people?

Did I just not matter in the face of this love, even though I had been the one to risk everything to show Rapunzel the world? Was I just supposed to fall on my sword because Eugene was uncomfortable that he didn't have every last piece of information about Rapunzel?

Thunder roared, as if echoing the anger in my chest. I opened my window and leaned out. The moon glowed between thick, shifting clouds. I called to Owl, and moments later he rested on my arm. Here was a friend: steady, true, and loyal.

It was all so unfair. *Why should I have to go?* A nagging voice in my head told me that I'd lived in Corona first. I'd grown up here. I liked it here. This was all I'd ever known. I could find the ancient power and master the Winged Beast and probably be captain one day. . . .

Don't listen to that voice, I told myself. *Stop being weak.* I had to make a decision. Waffling would get me nowhere.

"The plan is to leave tonight if the coast is clear," I said. Owl met my gaze with wise understanding. He narrowed his eyes, as if questioning me. "I'm not being rash. I know what I'm doing." Owl looked deep into my eyes. "Don't pull that staring into my soul stuff on me. You're just going to have to trust me. I can't go to a convent. I can't stay here. Time for the open road." Owl still refused to agree that running away was the best thing to do. "I'm going to pack."

Then lightning scratched the sky like an angry cat, and the rain started. Owl flew to a nearby tree for shelter. I flopped on my bed. It was a famous Coronan storm. Nature ruled.

No matter what I wanted, I was in Corona for another night.

18
RAPUNZEL

A loud clap of thunder shook the dining table. "Oh, my! It's a storm!" Marie, the Hervanian princess, exclaimed as she clasped her napkin.

"Yes," I said, thinking that I couldn't have asked for a better present. A storm would slow down Cass's departure, though not for long.

"A storm is the perfect time for reading," Monsieur LaFleur said, winking at me. Mom had invited him to join us because we were an odd number and she didn't want anyone to be left out of a dance. "And dancing!"

CHAPTER EIGHTEEN

"Our Rapunzel is a voracious reader," Mom said.

"Is that so?" the duchess asked.

"Yes, and she has an interest in ancient poetry," Monsieur LaFleur added.

"Is that true?" Mom asked.

I nodded. Exactly how long would a storm contain Cass? I wondered. One day? Two? How would I ever get her to stay?

"I hope my daughter always follows her passions. You must feel the same, Marquis?" Dad asked.

"Of course," the marquis said. "Marie is so sporty."

"And also has a keen interest in fashion," the duchess added. "She designed the very dress dear Rapunzel is wearing."

"Oh," I said. The puffed sleeves nearly reached my ears. "Thank you."

Marie nodded.

"What an awful lot you two have to talk about," Dad said. "Thank goodness you will have an entire week to get to know one another."

"Yes," I said, sipping my water. "Thank goodness."

I knew that Dad thought I would be best friends with Marie, but all she seemed to want to talk about so far was perfumes and face powders and the various styles of puffed sleeves that were so popular in Hervan. All I could think about was Cass. I couldn't imagine my life in Corona without her.

Another ominous clap of thunder sounded.

"Dear me!" shrieked the duchess. "Are we in danger?"

"No, we're safe," Mom said.

"Will you pass the quail pie?" asked the marquis, dabbing his lips with a napkin.

"I hope the rain won't deter our game of flying disk tomorrow," Marie said. "Flying disk is my favorite!"

"Never!" Mom said. "Rapunzel's lady-in-waiting, Cassandra, is very into sports. She'll be setting up our field come rain or shine!"

"Our Marie is quite the athlete," the duchess said.

"Athletes make the very best dancers," Monsieur LaFleur said. "No one appreciates the true athleticism of dance."

"I do, and I've won a few championships," Marie said.

More thunder roared. The duchess paled.

"Fear not. These Coronan storms come on strong but they depart as quickly as they arrive," Mom said. "I know we are all looking forward to some good fun tomorrow. Aren't we, Rapunzel?"

CHAPTER EIGHTEEN

"Oh, yes," I said, hoping that the storm wouldn't pass until morning. If Cass had a chance to leave under the cover of night, she'd take it. But then again, what if the storm didn't keep Cass there? What if, once she thought the book was safe, she departed anyway? I felt faint.

"Do you have an outfit for sports, Rapunzel?" Marie asked me, forcing me back to the moment.

"I usually just wear my regular dress," I said.

"I wear a low puff for sports. The full puff, as I have here on this gown, is the most royal look of all, don't you agree, Rapunzel?"

"Yes, the full puff is by far the best. Though, can you tell me one more time, which kind of puff is most appropriate for, say, a day by the seashore?" I asked, knowing she would spin off into a monologue about fashion, allowing me to return to my thoughts. I needed to accomplish three things: first, I had to get Cass to stay in Corona; second, I had to win her back; and finally, we needed to figure out the mystery of the lagoon—for the good of the kingdom.

At last, after the soup course, Mom asked if Eugene and I would like to show the Hervanian nobility the allemande dance we had been rehcarsing.

"Yes," I said, leaping to get away from the table and have some alone time with Eugene. I approached the musicians and whispered, "Can you make this a very, *very* long allemande?" The pianist winked and began to play.

"Eugene, what am I going to do? Cass wants to leave," I said as we began to dance.

"Would that really be the worst thing in the world?" Eugene asked.

"Yes," I said, giving his shoulder a squeeze.

"I'm sorry," he said, spinning me. "I was just kidding. I know Cassandra means the world to you." As he reeled me back into his arms and the Hervanian nobility offered a polite clap, Eugene whispered, "I promise I'll help you figure this out."

Normally, the dance might end there, but I nodded at the pianist, who started up again.

"What's her plan exactly?" Eugene asked.

"Just to leave," I said as we reset in the classical starting pose.

"Wow, she must be mad," he said.

"Yes, she thinks I've betrayed her," I said, stepping on his toes. "Oopsie." Eugene and I grinned at the marquis and his family.

"Life's not easy out on the road. Trust me, I've been there," Eugene said. "She's going to want to prep. I know for a fact that being a guard is hard."

"Cass is so tough," I said.

"But she's been a lady-in-waiting for six months," he said as we turned a rosette. "That's not exactly training."

"That's it!" I said. "There's this move she wants to learn. Maybe I can convince her to stay long enough to learn it, and then she'll trust me again. Oh, Eugene, I adore you!" Forgetting myself, I kissed his cheek, and the duchess gasped.

"She is so swept up in the art of dance," Mom said, covering for me.

"I can hardly blame them," the duchess said, fanning herself. "The allemande is most romantic."

"Shall we all dance?" Dad asked Mom.

"How could I refuse?" Mom answered.

And the musicians began again. Eugene and I spun off, Mom and Dad held hands, the marquis and the duchess bowed to one another, and Monsieur LaFleur extended his hand to Marie.

"Who is that?" Marie asked the next day when we arrived at the sports field for our early morning game of flying disk. Sure enough, Marie had the best flying disk outfit, replete with a low puffed sleeve and a matching headband.

"That's my lady-in-waiting, Cassandra," I said, unable to contain my smile. She had stayed! Though I'd guessed she had when I'd returned to my room to see the book of poems replaced by a note in her hand that stated simply: *I've got it.*

"She looks, um, formidable," Marie said, and began to stretch her calves.

"Oh, she is," Eugene said. I nudged him. "In the best way, of course. By 'formidable' I mean in the sense of 'impressive.' I'd never call her, say, 'difficult' or, even worse, 'menacing.'"

I shot Eugene a look and then waved to Cass.

She reluctantly waved back as if to say, *Yes, I'm still here, but don't get used to it.* As Marie led everyone in stretching exercises on one end of the arena, I went to greet Cassandra at the other.

"Do you have the book?" I asked.

"Of course," she said, preparing the field. She was placing painted rocks on the ground to outline the boundaries. "It's in my satchel right there. But I'm returning it to you after this game. I'm leaving tonight. That's the end of it."

"Even though Monsieur LaFleur wanted it?" I asked. "That has to be a sign, a clue, that we have something valuable here."

"Cassandra is one of the best flying disk players

in the kingdom," Mom said, calling to us from across the field.

Cassandra nodded and waved. "Yeah, I admit it's weird. But it's not going to stop me from going."

"We'll have two teams of four!" my father declared. "The Hervanians versus the Coronans. Though one of us will have to play for the other side."

"I nominate Cassandra!" Eugene shouted.

"You're going to regret that, Fitzherbert," Cassandra called back.

"Are you really prepared to leave Corona?" I asked Cass as she walked heel to toe, measuring the playing field. "Don't you think you should train before you set out? Don't you think there are certain things you should know?"

Cass paused, biting her lip. I had given her something to think about. But then she seemed to shake the idea off. "I'll be fine. I grew up among the guards. I'm sure I can handle myself wherever I land."

"You've been my lady-in-waiting for more than six months," I said. "It's seriously cut into your physical conditioning. I know you don't want to be out on the road without a top-notch skill set. Let me help you."

"The playing field seems like it is defined," Dad called. "Let's get this game started. Take your places, girls."

Friedborg blew a whistle.

"Wait!" Marie cried, running to the other end of the field. "I forgot my lucky armband."

"Why should I trust you, anyway?" Cass asked.

"Because you have no choice. How else are you going to prepare for a life on the road? You can't *really* fence with yourself. You can't chase yourself up castle walls. And it'll be totally undercover. It's your job to hang out with me, right?" I asked. She nodded. "But instead of teaching me embroidery, lute playing, and the art of elevated conversation, we'll be getting you ready to be the best guard this world has ever seen." I paused. "We could learn the Winged Beast. We didn't have time before. But we could make it a priority now."

Her eyes lit up. I had her!

"Ready!" Marie cried, sliding a brightly colored piece of fabric that perfectly matched her headband onto her arm.

"Cassandra, take your place with the Hervanians," Eugene said.

"Calm down, Eugene," she said.

"I'll guard Cass!" I said, standing next to her.

CHAPTER EIGHTEEN

"I'll stay until after the Hidden Moon Festival," she said, gazing at the horizon. *Yes!* That was in ten days! "Maybe we can find out more about the lagoon, too. . . . But after that, I'm leaving, Rapunzel. And until then, if Eugene breathes a word—"

"He won't," I said.

"Is it just me, or are we missing something?" Eugene asked as we all stood in position.

"The disk!" Marie exclaimed.

"It's in my bag," Cass said. She ran to get it. But when she returned with the disk, her face was stricken.

"What is it?" I asked.

"The book," she said. "It's missing."

19

CASSANDRA

"**W**hat was the last place you had the book?" Raps asked me as I collected the painted rocks that marked the boundaries of the field. She was red-faced after our game of flying disk, which was more competitive than we'd expected.

Eugene and I had played as though we were fighting for Corona's honor, matching each other point for point with snipes, bullet passes, and air benders. It was hardly a one-on-one game, though. The fastest runner on the field was Raps, and she'd held her own, foot-blocking the Hervanian marquis and catching Eugene's long passes pancake-style. But at the last minute, the Hervanians and I beat the Coronans. That Marie was tougher than she looked under her puffy sleeves. She'd scored the winning point with an aggressive run and battle-tackle that surprised us all.

Now, as the rest of the group headed back to the castle, Raps and I hung back to talk privately.

"What do you mean, what was the last place I had it?" I asked. "It was in my satchel this morning. I wasn't about to leave it in my room with LaFleur nosing around."

"Did you at any point leave it alone, or have you been with it the whole time?" Raps asked.

"Since when do I leave my stuff just lying around?" I asked, annoyed.

"Sorry," Raps said, hands in the air. "I was just asking. Do you think . . . ? Would the Hervanians?"

We looked at Marie, who was wiping the mud from her shoes. It seemed unlikely, but then again, so had her tackle point. Plus, she had headed in the direction of my satchel when she went to get her lucky armband. It was possible. . . .

"They're seeking Coronan protection, but you never know. Maybe that's just a guise, and they're really after power. We'll add them to the list of suspects. In the meantime, let's interview LaFleur."

It took us very little time to locate the dance instructor. He was in the great hall, where he was directing the national dance troupe in rehearsals for their performance at the Hidden Moon Festival.

"Rise together, my doves, and follow me as we lead the revolution!" Monsieur LaFleur was saying to the group of at least fifty dancers on the stage as the pianist played with passion. He waved his hands above him and the dancers copied him. Behind them, carpenters were taking measurements and decorators were painting sets depicting all the flowers that bloom in the springtime in Corona.

"Revolution? What kind of dance is this?" I asked Raps as we made our way toward the stage. The dancers were twirling wildly, leaping and bounding with feverish looks in their eyes. Was LaFleur a madman? Was this "dance troupe" his army of crazed minions?

"I think they're just . . . dancing?" Raps said.

I stuck four fingers in my mouth and gave my loudest whistle. The piano music stopped, the dancers froze, and everyone turned and looked at me.

"Hey!" I yelled. "What's going on in here?"

Monsieur LaFleur eyed us with shock. His cheeks were pink with either shame or exertion—or perhaps both.

"Princess! Madamoiselle Cassandra! I wasn't expecting you," LaFleur said with a weird grin as he quickly made his way down the stage stairs.

"Clearly not," I said. "What kind of *revolution* is going on here?"

"Dancers, take five," Monsieur LaFleur said, flustered. He dabbed his perspiration-soaked forehead with a hanky. The dancers whispered among themselves as Monsieur LaFleur cleared his throat and joined us.

"Hi," Raps said. "Um, can you explain this?"

"I have an unorthodox creative method," LaFleur said nervously. "Is that . . . a crime?"

"Of course not," Raps said. "Every artist is entitled to his or her own process."

"But you were talking about a revolution," I said. Raps might have been willing to let him off the hook, but I wasn't.

"A revolution of the soul," LaFleur said. "How can I create a dance worthy of a Hidden Moon Festival if I don't stir the passions of my dancers? When was the last Hidden Moon Festival? Fifty years ago? Our light source will be in shadows! Our dreams will be smothered. What does that mean? And what, by the way, does it mean to be human? These are the questions I'm asking in order to create a dance for such an auspicious moment in time."

"Cass, I think he's being honest," Raps said.

"What about the book of poems? Did you take it?" I asked.

"It's missing," Raps said.

"Oh, dear. Take it? Without permission? I'd never do such a thing," LaFleur said, looking genuinely offended. "The princess said it was too important to her. Though I do hope you reconsider, if you find it. My life's dream has been to write a ballet about 'The Lost Lagoon' and then take it on the road, travel the world with a message of love! If I had the original text, why, I could dive right into it, so to speak."

"There's no need for puns," I said, staring straight into his eyes. Raps was right. He exhibited no traits of a liar, though I wasn't quite prepared to let him off the hook.

"I know who took it!" LaFleur said suddenly, his eyes lighting up.

"Who?" Raps asked.

"My archrival and former paramour, Louisa Von

Almond!" he cried out. "Long ago, I shared with her my vision of a ballet about 'The Lost Lagoon.' She's stolen my idea! She'll be a runaway success, and I'll wither away in obscurity, and she'll love every moment of it!"

"I don't think the book was stolen to make a ballet," Raps said. "Though if that was the case, I'm not sure I'd mind. . . ."

"You don't know Louisa," LaFleur said. "She's a rose of few petals and many thorns."

"I think you'd better get back to your dancers," Raps said.

"For now," I added sternly.

"Art first!" Monsieur LaFleur exclaimed, and then he clapped his hands to indicate the break was over. He wasn't a *prime* suspect, but he wasn't off the list, either. I mean, was Louisa Von Almond even a real name?

The Hervanians weren't anywhere to be found, so Raps and I decided to head straight to the lagoon to search for more clues—or any evidence that someone had been there.

While Raps investigated one side of the lagoon, I explored the other. I challenged myself to swim to the far wall of the lagoon, which formed a cove. We didn't go over there much because it was farthest from the gulch and rarely got any sun. It was the one spot in the lagoon that was usually dark.

The water became colder the closer I got to the cove. We had been looking for other gems, and nothing sparkled in this area. I couldn't keep my eyes open underwater for very long, so I used my other senses, according to guard training. I ran my hand along the wall. It all felt normal . . . until it didn't. Then there was a break, and the stone was uneven. Something was etched in its side. I forced my eyes open and saw words. I swam to the surface.

"I found something," I said. "Raps, come here!"

Rapunzel dove into the lagoon and swam right over.

"Check it out," I said. "It's hard to read, but I think it's Saporian."

"What? This is amazing!" She inhaled deeply and dove under. When she came back up, she said, "We're just going to have to take it word by word. I'll get my diary. You read the letters to me; I'll write them down."

"Got it," I said. Raps raced back to the shore while I pushed myself to go back underwater. This was a clue to the greatest power Corona had. I could feel it the way a bull shark could anticipate its prey. We were getting close.

After multiple dives and alternating roles, Raps and I had a sentence: *Ackoui rescede o oure treasure, ligaro comme an embrace, nayo dixie que sejir disturbe.*

We focused on the words we thought we understood—*treasure, embrace, disturb*—but we still couldn't divine the meaning. We repeated the sentence so many times that by the time we headed back to the castle, we'd memorized it.

20

RAPUNZEL

"Inside of each of us is a burning flame," Miss Tasha the matchmaker explained in her low, smooth voice. "When two flames who are meant to be come together, one must wonder: will they blend, or cast two different shadows? This is the question matchmakers must answer, and we do it by viewing the auras of those around us." The lights were dimmed and the curtains were drawn in the parlor room, which was one of the few quiet places in the castle.

It was a few days after our last visit to the lagoon, and Cass and I were busy trying to line up experts for the Hidden Moon Festival, which was taking more time than we had expected. Mom had told me that a record number of engagements happened after the Hidden Moon Festival—the villagers depended on it—so I had better line up a matchmaker who was worth her salt. Miss Tasha, it was rumored, was the best in the land. She had come to the castle to give us a demonstration.

In the meantime, my mother was running around overseeing the planning for the many educational programs. My father was working with the guards to ensure top security. Eugene, in charge of the entertainment lineup, was busy interviewing bands that might perform in the great hall in advance of LaFleur's dance finale.

"How long do you think this is going to take?" Cass whispered. "We need to keep working on our translations."

"I don't know. I've never seen a matchmaker in action before," I whispered back. "Do *you* think she's any good?"

"Can't tell," Cass said. "This isn't my bag."

Miss Tasha nodded to the lute player, who was seated behind us in the shadows so that, as Miss Tasha had told us, his physical presence wouldn't distract from his music.

"Now I shall demonstrate my technique. Close

your eyes," Miss Tasha said in a soothing voice. "And let us quiet our minds so that our inner beings can resonate with the vibrations of the lute. With open hearts and clear heads, I can see the colors of people's hearts and find their perfect complement."

"What a loon," Cass whispered.

"So it's something something 'our treasure' something 'with an embrace,' then something about 'don't disturb' . . ." I whispered. The previous night we'd scoured the few Saporian books we'd found in the library in an attempt to translate the words carved on the wall of the lagoon, but this was as far as we'd gotten. Kinnaird, the ancient librarian, wasn't there, so we couldn't ask him about the visitor who'd been inquiring about the stolen book. Kinnaird kept odd hours.

"Ladies, I do hate to be rude," Miss Tasha said. "But I hear chitter-chatter. I can't do my best work without a bit of focus, eh?"

"Sorry," I said.

We closed our eyes and listened to the lute player until Miss Tasha spoke.

"The vibrations in the room are humming. I will bring in some citizens of the castle, and tell you the color of their auras and if, perhaps, there is a match among us here today."

"I'm ready," I said.

"This is some weird stuff," Cass said.

Miss Tasha opened the door. Eugene walked in. I smiled.

"Pfff," Cass said.

"My, my," Miss Tasha said. "Rapunzel's aura is ablaze—the most vivid purple hue! And dear Eugene's is a bright orange, with flecks of pure gold."

Eugene beamed.

"Are you serious?" Cass asked, leaning back in her chair. "I don't see anything except . . . Fitzherbert."

"That's really neat," I said, grinning.

"You're a perfect match," Miss Tasha said, her hands clasped to her chest. "Your auras align on the color wheel to perfection."

"Awwww, sweet," I said.

"Sunshine, did you ever doubt we were meant to be?" Eugene asked with a grin.

"Never," I said.

"Don't you two ever get bored of this ooey-gooey stuff?" Cassandra asked.

"Captain Bitter, you have a lot to learn," Eugene replied.

"If I were chosen to make matches at the Hidden Moon Festival, I would ensure they were all as solid as this," Miss Tasha said with a curtsy.

"Ugh," Cassandra muttered.

"The mood! The mood! It's turning sour," Miss Tasha said, covering her ears. "It's affecting the other auras. Eugene's is darkening with every passing second. I must ask you to leave so that any superfluous tension dissipates in this room. As for you, Cassandra, it would behoove you to be more softhearted and, *ahem*, obedient. That is, if you'd like me to help you find love."

"I think I'll pass," Cassandra said. Miss Tasha scowled. I nudged Cass, and she looked at me as if to say, *What?*

"Lute player, clear our minds with a pleasing tune!" Miss Tasha said.

The lute player bowed his head and started up again.

"Is it just me, or does that lute player seem familiar?" Cass lowered her voice, squinting to see him in the shadows.

"I can't get a clear view," I whispered back.

"Well, anyway, I think we need to go back to Xavier and see if we can get a Saporian dictionary," Cass said.

"Good idea," I said.

CHAPTER TWENTY

"*Ahem!* Next up," Miss Tasha said. Friedborg walked in.

"She has an aura?" Cass asked.

Friedborg frowned.

"Of course she does, Cass," I said, wondering if the quietest people were perhaps the most sensitive.

"Yes, she has an aura. In fact—it's a red flame! A sign of deep romance. Friedborg, you are yearning for love!" Miss Tasha exclaimed. Friedborg blushed wildly. "Your match will have a green flame. To soothe your passionate heart."

"This lady is nutso," Cass said.

"I guess there's more to Friedborg than meets the eye," I said.

"Tomorrow," Cass said, "when we're done with this nonsense—"

"It's not nonsense. It's all for the festival!" I said. "And think about how great it would be if Friedborg found a sweetheart!"

"We'll see Xavier first thing," Cass replied.

"Do you think he knows how to translate Saporian?" I asked.

"If anyone does, it's Xavier," Cass said.

The lute player seemed to find more energy and passion as Friedborg left and Miss Tasha's third candidate walked into the room. It was Marie the Hervanian.

"Marie," Cass said, standing up and suddenly serious. "We've been meaning to ask you something—"

We'd been wondering more and more if the Hervanians might have had something to do with the book's disappearance—especially after I'd remembered that Monsieur LaFleur had referenced my interest in ancient poetry in front of them during our dinner. But I wasn't sure now was the best time or place to probe for information.

"What is that?" Marie asked.

"You don't have any interest in poetry, do you?" Cass asked.

"Cass . . ." I said.

"I don't understand your line of questioning, Cassandra," Miss Tasha said. "It's distracting Marie's mind and taking her away from the present moment. I think I see her aura! It's blue!"

"We need to interrogate you!" Cass said.

"I must ask the lady-in-waiting to leave the room!" Miss Tasha announced. "I beg of you, Princess. I cannot work under these . . . unfriendly . . . conditions!"

"Cass?" I asked.

"Fine, fine," Cass said. "I have work to do anyway."

CHAPTER TWENTY

"I'll see you after?" I asked Cass.

"Marie, you are a daring woman with so much to give," Miss Tasha said. "Your match will be a complicated soul, but one with the highest intentions!"

I waved to Cass as she left the room.

21

CASSANDRA

The marquis and duchess were riding horses through the kingdom, and I knew that Marie was having her aura examined down in the parlor. The guards were running various emergency exercises in anticipation of the Hidden Moon Festival. And Raps, who would probably try to stop me from breaking in because it wasn't "the honest thing to do," was tied up learning how to look at people's inner flames or whatever nonsense Miss Tasha was spouting.

In other words, it was the perfect time to do some investigating.

My palms tingled in anticipation as I jimmied the

lock and turned the large doorknob on the heavy door of the guest chambers. I winced as the door creaked. Then I slipped inside, shutting the door behind me. Marie could have easily stolen the book at the field. Though, I had to admit, if she had taken it, she was one of the greatest deceivers of all time. The girl didn't appear to be much smarter or wilier than a bucket of dust. In any case, it was time to find out.

I rifled through Marie's belongings. *Jeez.* This girl had more dresses than Raps. She had outfits for every imaginable occasion, from teatime to jousting to weight lifting. Each ensemble was labeled and paired with a matching headband. Maybe she was some kind of evil genius? There was a system here.

She was so organized it didn't take long to go through her things. There was no sign of the book and no evidence that pointed to any knowledge of the lagoon. And yet . . . I had to wonder. *Do people really live this way? With labeled socks for every day of the week?* She was clearly deranged.

I hated to admit it, but I understood for a moment why Eugene might have liked being a thief. There was an undeniable excitement in being somewhere I wasn't supposed to be. Though, unlike

Eugene, my thieving efforts were in the name of justice. Who knew why Eugene did anything— well, except for love . . . or whatever.

We had considered Marie a suspect, though of course her parents were just as likely to have taken the book. I turned my attention to the gilded travel trunks of the marquis and the duchess. With fast fingers, I searched for the book. One thing was certain. The duchess had enough jewels to *fill* the lagoon. I didn't know why she'd go in search of more.

At last I came across something that felt like our long-lost book of poetry.

It was tucked beneath some underclothes. I grabbed the leather-bound book, opening its pages with bated breath.

However, it turned out to be a diary kept by the marquis, which seemed to revolve mostly around eating.

> *5 February. I ate the rest of the plum pudding for breakfast. I hope my wife doesn't find out or she will be sore!*
> *10 March. Had a hunk of ham with a loaf of brown bread for dinner. Perhaps I overindulged? Indigestion seems inevitable. Sad face.*

CHAPTER TWENTY-ONE

2 April. Pie, pie, pie. Mince, squash, and apple.
I sampled them all at the feast today, yet
still missed Mother's blueberry crumble.
Will anything ever come close to its
deliciousness?

Boy, this guy needed some hobbies.

"Excuse me, what are you doing?" Marie asked. I
tried to appear neutral, even though my heart was
pounding and she'd caught me red-handed reading her father's journal!

"Extermination!" I said with a smile.

"Excuse me?" Marie said, her hands folded across
her chest.

"We've had an infestation and it seems to be
originating from this room. We're wondering: did
they travel from Hervan?" I said. Marie narrowed
her eyes. "Obviously, I had to investigate if any
bugs arrived via Hervanian luggage."

She wrinkled her nose.

"Spiders," I said, improvising.

"We have no spiders in our luggage!" Marie said,
taking great offense.

"I can see that now," I said, quickly putting back
the journal. "And I'll be sure to end the vicious
rumors that are circulating."

"I should hope so!" Marie said. "I should have you reported to the queen!"

"Unless, of course, you'd like to participate in the biggest event of the festival," I said, thinking on my feet.

Marie eyed me skeptically. "Of what do you speak?"

"Would you like to fence with Rapunzel? As a way to kick off the celebration?"

"Me? Fence with the princess? In front of the entire kingdom?" she asked, brightening.

"Absolutely!" I said. "Without a challenger of physical prowess, it will just be a joke. But a truly skilled and yet friendly fencing match? Why the townspeople will be talking about it for ages."

"When can we begin practicing?" Marie asked.

"Just as soon as possible," I replied. "I'm going to go check in with the princess now."

"Wonderful. I'll make sure my fencing gear is ready!"

"Why exactly am I doing this?" Raps asked me as I fastened her headpiece.

"Diplomacy," I said. "Besides, we had to kick off the ceremonies somehow."

"I guess," Raps said.

CHAPTER TWENTY-ONE

Marie was nearby performing an elaborate warm-up routine. I wondered if I'd missed anything in my search. Yes, they were our allies. But if history had taught me anything, it was that the smallest countries almost always had the largest ambitions.

"I thought we were going to Xavier's today. And what about the Winged Beast?" Raps said.

"Look, I needed to search the Hervanians' guest quarters . . ." I said.

"You broke in?" Raps asked.

I shrugged. "She was the only one who'd actually been near my satchel that morning. I had to rule them out."

"Well?" Raps asked as I pinned the loose strands of her braid.

"I couldn't find evidence of a direct motivation, but they aren't ruled out yet."

"So what's my job?" she asked.

"Fight like heck," I said, fastening her chin strap. "Everyone loves a fencing match."

"I'm glad you're the one who trained me!" Raps said as Marie performed a double backflip with sword in hand.

"Hi ya! I'm ready!" Marie said. "You think that because my country is little, it is not mighty" She pulled a double-triple backward revenge move. "You are wrong. The humblest among us have the greatest thirst for power." Rapunzel and I glanced at each other, taking in what she'd just said. Then Marie advanced. "En garde!"

"Eek!" Rapunzel cried, but quickly rebounded, blocking Marie's parry.

22

RAPUNZEL

"That fencing match made me really hungry," I said later as Cass and I walked to the village on our way to see Xavier. Once again, the scent of those pastries made my mouth water. "I sure could use a pastry to give me a boost in energy."

"We're on a mission," Cass said. She was still resolute about leaving after the festival, but I knew her well enough to know there was a smile hiding inside her right now. I just needed to draw it out.

"The most important mission ever," I said. "And we need fuel."

"In the form of sugar and cream?" Cass asked.

"What better fuel could there be?" I asked. I held her arm as we passed the door of the baker's shop. "Stop. Inhale."

"Ugh. Fine," Cassandra said. *There* was that semblance of a smile.

"I knew you'd come around," I said with a grin.

"This is going to be fast," she said.

"So fast," I said. "Faster than Marie and her counter ripostes."

"Marie isn't ordinary nobility—she's a warrior," Cass said. "Who knows if she's even royalty at all. She could be a trained assassin."

"But those outfits . . ." I said.

"Doesn't mean a thing," Cass said. "Elaborate disguises have been used for lesser evils."

"If what you described to me about her wardrobe is accurate, that's an awful lot of headbands to convince us of a false identity," I said. Cass's brow furrowed as she considered this. If Marie and I were a match for fencing, Cass and I were perfectly paired for thinking problems through. "Cass, you can't leave the kingdom. You just can't!"

She snapped out of her private thoughts. "I can, actually. And I have to. There's no life for me here. You know as well as I do I can't risk your parents finding out I snuck you out of the kingdom."

CHAPTER TWENTY-TWO

"But Corona needs you," I said. "And I do, too."

"I'll do my duty until after the festival," she said coldly. My heart sank. Just a moment ago, she'd felt like my best friend again. Now she was all business. "The guard should keep an extra eye on Marie. In the event that she's being dishonest, she might choose any moment to lead a Hervanian revolution—and if they know about the lagoon, we'll be at serious risk."

"I'm going to rebel if I don't have something to eat," I said, trying to reel her back in with my humor.

"Fine, fine," Cass said. "But then we go straight to Xavier's."

"Of course," I said.

She sighed and went into the baker's shop.

I saw Dahlia, the paint seller, setting up a display. I looked back and forth from Cassandra in the baker's window to Dahlia, who was adjusting the frame of what appeared to be her own work of art before she stepped back and evaluated it. Energy buzzed through me—I had an idea! I needed to paint something for Cass! Something that would remind her of all our good times together! We'd been working so well together for the past few days. I still had hope that I could get through to her. Art communicated when words failed. It could convey emotion without sentiment. I could use my paintbrush to speak a language that Cass might actually understand. Maybe language wasn't the key. If I could get the picture just right, she would know how important she was to Corona and to me. And I could present it to her at the Hidden Moon Festival.

"Excuse me," I said, approaching Dahlia.

"Oh, hi!" she said.

Her warm, genuine smile put me immediately at ease. I noticed that her canvas had an almost completed painting on it. It depicted the castle in all its glory. It was full of village folks dressed in their finest attire and making the most of life. Dahlia's work was rich with detail. I spotted vendors proudly showing off their wares, children playing hide-and-seek in the castle gardens, and gardeners gesturing to their verdant arrangements. Most poignantly, she'd captured the faces of an older couple as they danced in the courtyard, and for a moment I lost my breath.

"Is that . . . the Hidden Moon Festival?" I asked.

She bit her lip and nodded.

I gazed at it. The scene was intimate and lively, and made me feel just a little bit closer to Corona.

"My parents met and fell in love at this festival," Dahlia said.

"Really?" I asked, a hand to my heart. I guess it was true what Mom had said about the villagers finding romance this time of year.

"Uh-huh," she said, smiling. "And every year, my whole family spends days getting ready. We sew our outfits by hand. This year we'll all be in white to represent the hidden moon."

"That will be so beautiful," I said. "Of course, I've never been to it."

"You'll love it," she said. "It brings out the best in everybody. The chefs, the artists, the gardeners, the musicians, the dancers. It's like, there's nowhere else you'd rather be, you know?"

"Yes!" I said, feeling a genuine excitement for what had seemed like another princess obligation.

I gathered my courage and said, "I was actually wondering if you might want to help me." Her face lit up. "There's a special project I'd like to do. It's very personal."

"I'd love that!" Dahlia said. "It'd be a dream come true. I've always been a bystander at the festival. But to actually help the princess with a special project. Wow."

"Oh, good," I said, smiling because her enthusiasm was contagious. "But it's kind of a secret, okay?"

"Mum's the word," Dahlia said, her eyes shining.

"I'm so glad we had a chance to talk," I said. "Come by the castle tomorrow. We'll be painting backdrops for the dance—a perfect cover for our real mission."

"Raps!" Cass called from in front of the bakery.

"I have to go," I said, waving as I walked away. "See you tomorrow."

"What were you doing?" Cass asked, handing me my pastry as I joined her.

"Asking Dahlia to display her expertise at the Hidden Moon Festival," I said.

"I already told you, the royal portrait painter does that," Cass said. "Everyone who displays needs to be vetted."

"We can vet her tomorrow," I said.

"We have to stay on task," Cass said again. This time there was no smile under her voice.

"I just have one more question," I said to Xavier. I pulled out my diary and showed him the phrase we'd read on the wall. "What does this mean?"

Xavier studied the Saporian words. "'Herein lies

our treasure, bonded with an embrace; let it not be disturbed.' Where did you find this?"

"In another book," Cassandra said. "Rapunzel here is such a bookworm!"

I shrugged and smiled.

"Isn't Saporian a beautiful language?" Xavier said. I nodded.

Luckily, in addition to "The Lost Lagoon," I'd copied a few of the other poems from the green book into my diary.

"Can you translate the other poems for us—the ones in Saporian?" I asked.

"I'd rather give you the tools to translate it yourself. I'm sure you'll find that to be a much more satisfying experience. I'm so glad our returned princess has a love of languages. I'll have Marco deliver those books as soon as possible—they are buried deep in my storage trunks, so it may take until tomorrow."

"That would be great," I said. "Thanks for everything."

Just then Marco came out of the back room. "The dagger has been perfected, Xavier."

"And just in time for security for the Hidden Moon Festival," Xavier said.

"Can I see it?" Cass asked.

"Be careful, young lady," Marco said. "That's a *very* dangerous object you're holding. It's the thinnest, strongest blade on any continent."

"Marco ought to know," Xavier said. "He's a world traveler. Arrived here just a month ago from across the Silodeen Sea, where he apprenticed the king's guard."

"I have plenty of experience with daggers," Cass said, narrowing her eyes at a spot on the wall. "So you don't need to worry about me."

"She's the daughter of the captain of the guard," I said. I didn't like the way Marco had assumed Cass might not know her weapons.

Cass made a swift motion with her hand, tossing the dagger with an expert's aim. *Whoosh.* We watched the dagger land with its blade in the doorframe.

Xavier whistled in admiration.

"Not bad at all!" Marco said. "You've clearly been practicing for years."

"Didn't you try out for the Coronan guard, Marco?" Xavier asked.

Marco blanched for a moment but cleared his throat and said, "Yes, though I knew it wasn't the place for me."

"Why is that?" Cass asked, her head cocked in

interest. "Our guard is the best in the world."

"I suppose I've learned over the years that understanding one's weaknesses is the gateway to true strength," he said with a sigh. Xavier nodded. I could see why these two worked together.

"What do you mean?" Cass asked.

"I have always wanted to be a defender of the kingdom," Marco continued. "But alas, I wasn't built for it. Bravery, physical prowess, and coordination just aren't my talents."

"They are mine," Cass said.

"Clearly," Xavier said, removing the dagger from the doorframe.

"But I'm not allowed to join the guard," Cass said.

"Not now, maybe," Marco said. "The one thing we can count on is change." Cass almost grinned. Something gave color to her cheeks, and I guessed it was hope.

"As for me, I knew I'd never rise above the rank of apprentice," Marco said.

"What are *your* true talents?" I asked.

Marco smiled and tapped his head. "Me, I'm a thinker. I hunger for knowledge above all. History is like a never-ending puzzle to me. Language is a universe of wonder."

"And you're handy with the welding iron, as

well," Xavier said with a chuckle, "which helps in this position."

"True, true," Marco said. "This is the best of all worlds. Working for you, the wisest and most knowledgeable man in all of Corona, is clearly where I belong."

"I'd like one of those daggers someday," Cass said.

"Then I'm sure you'll have one," Marco said. "Just maybe not when you expect it—destiny is a fickle fairy. But as long as we pursue our dreams, she eventually will let us catch her. And then—then, my dears—when we are living our dreams, the world is ours."

23

CASSANDRA

Since Marco wasn't scheduled to deliver the books until that evening, Raps insisted we go to the lagoon to practice the Winged Beast, which I appreciated. But what I had told Raps that afternoon was still true: I was leaving. Even if the mystery of the lagoon tugged at me like an encouraging hand, pulling me back. There was no way I was going to live in fear of being sent away or labeled as untrustworthy. That would make it impossible for me to pursue a life of dignity and service.

Marco's words about destiny echoed in my mind. I would not play it safe. I would hold fast to my dream of living a life of adventure and freedom. I would never give up on joining a guard—even if it meant not being part of the *Coronan* one.

We were in the shady glade of the lagoon. I opened *The Ultimate Warrior Handbook* and pointed to the diagram labeled THE WINGED BEAST and said, "This is the move that will set me apart from all the others."

"Looks . . . complicated," Raps said. She took a deep breath. "But we can do it if we try!"

I handed the book to her and stretched out my hamstrings as she began to read.

"'The Winged Beast has only been performed by the highest level of warrior. It is said that soldiers who are able to execute this highly sophisticated maneuver have reached a level of mastery.' Jeez," she said, turning the book sideways to see the illustration from another angle. "No wonder it's so impressive. This is some serious gymnastics."

"So, you don't think you can help me?" I asked.

"I didn't say that," she said. "We'll get to work on it right now. I think you're going to have to get on my shoulders."

"You'll be getting on *my* shoulders," I said. "I'll be the base, and you'll be the wings."

"If you say so," she said. She kept reading: "'The

strength comes from the soldier who serves as the base, while the one who operates as the wings must completely surrender his or her life to his or her partner.'" Raps paused and bit her lip. "Um, surrender her *life*?"

"If you land the wrong way you'll break your neck," I said. "If it wasn't life-threatening, it wouldn't be the ultimate warrior move, would it?" Raps nodded. "What, do you not trust me?"

"Of course I do," she said.

I waited a good three seconds before I started laughing. "I'm teasing you, Raps! You have your hair as a backup!"

"Oh!" she said, exhaling with relief.

"I got you so good!" I said as we both laughed.

"With anyone else, they'd be trusting me with their life; but you can wrap your hair around a branch so you're not in danger of hitting the ground. But you were really going to do it, weren't you?"

"I was," she admitted. "I was scared, but I was."

This wasn't nothing to me. She was loyal in most things. And we had been having fun lately. . . .

After we both stretched, we got to work. It took a few minutes to get into position.

"And on the count of three, I'm going to use

my hands to propel your foot upward," I said to Rapunzel.

We practiced again and again to no avail, but I was determined to at least master the first step of the Winged Beast. The entire move involved two soldiers appearing as a single person, with one hiding behind the other. Then, while the "base" distracted the enemy, the "wings" climbed on the base's back, wielding a knife. In a fast and fearless move, the base then flung the wings into the air, giving the wings the latitude to flip, flying toward the unsuspecting enemy headfirst, knocking him unconscious. The trick was that the base then had to catch the wings before she landed on her head, as the risk of major injury was high. Rapunzel's hair wrapped around a tree branch took most of the danger out of it, but it was still pretty scary to release her into the air. One wrong move and she could injure herself. The only way to pull off the move was for the wings to fall headfirst with total trust.

"I think you need to fling me a little higher," Raps said, swinging from the tree by her hair after the tenth or eleventh try. "I can't seem to get enough air to fall facedown."

CHAPTER TWENTY-THREE

"We can keep building upper-arm strength," I said.

"The book says it's all about alignment, though," Rapunzel said as she climbed up her hair to the tree branch so she could untangle herself from its limbs.

"Then I guess we'll have to align better next time," I said, wiping sweat from my brow. I had to admit, this was exhausting.

"Let's go for a swim before we go back to the castle," she said. "Maybe we'll find more hidden notes."

"We only have a few minutes, though," I said. "And your mom asked me yesterday why we're both so tan."

"What did you tell her?" Raps said as she freed herself and jumped back down to the ground.

"I said you just couldn't get enough of Coronan flora and fauna, and that—"

"Hey, this is a cool rock," Raps said suddenly.

"Oh, can I see that?" I asked.

"Sure," she said, handing it over.

"This isn't a rock," I said. "It's a relic. A genuine spearhead. And it belonged to nobility."

"How can you tell?" she asked.

"The shape of it, and the markings right here.

But it's missing the tip. Look, it's soft where it should be the sharpest. That's really odd."

"Are you sure it's not just a stone?" she asked.

"I'm sure. Check out these lines. They were definitely carved in."

"I know there are some books about military history back in the library," Raps said. "And this will definitely give us a clue about who's been here before."

I had a moment then as we were walking back—an idea that I should stay in Corona. That Rapunzel and I had work to do together. Long-term work. But I couldn't live with knowing that I could very well be banished at any moment. So I tossed the thought aside, holding the spearhead tightly in my fist.

24

RAPUNZEL

"So you're looking for books about old weapons, eh?" asked the ancient librarian, Kinnaird. He had a trim white beard, a smile that made his whole face crinkle up, and glasses that balanced on the end of a noble nose. It was the next morning, and Cass and I had decided to stop by during Kinnaird's working hours in case he could help us.

"Yes," I said.

"Spearheads, specifically," Cass said.

"I'm afraid that our weapons selection is limited," Kinnaird said, handing us three volumes. "But perhaps one of these books will be useful?"

"Are you prepared for the Hidden Moon Festival?" I asked him while Cass searched through the books.

"I'm as busy as can be," he said. "I'm giving a lecture on rare books, leading a bookbinding workshop, and holding a storytelling hour for the children."

"That sounds fun!" I said. "What book are you going to read them?"

"A Flynn Rider story would be appropriate, don't you think?" he asked.

"Absolutely!" I said, knowing instantly that Eugene wouldn't miss that for the world.

"I'm a bit behind, however. The library has been busier than normal," Kinnaird said as he gestured to books that needed to be reshelved.

"Lots of people preparing for the festival?" Cass asked, suddenly alert.

"Yes. I've had a lot of patrons—some I recognize, some I do not. That dance instructor, LaFleur, has been in many times searching the geography section, and our visitor, Marie of Hervan, is an avid reader of Coronan history."

"She is?" I asked, locking eyes with Cass.

"In fact, she has some overdue fines. I hate to be a bother," Kinnaird said. "But perhaps you could ever-so-subtly remind her of this if you see her?"

"That won't be a problem," Cass said, bringing the books to the counter to check them out.

"In fact, we're seeing her shortly," I said.

"Hmmm . . . There was nothing in those about this oddly shaped spearhead," I said as we made our way to the great hall. It was time to suit up for fencing practice.

"It has to be *something*," Cass said, turning the spearhead over in her hands. "Could it be one of the precious stones? Is this whole poem about the military?"

"Well, this spearhead doesn't exactly sparkle," I said. "It's just a rock in a certain shape. We explored every inch of that cove on our last visit. The only stones that seem precious are these—at least, when the sun shines on them."

I lifted my hand to reveal the bracelet. Cass stared at her own wrist. Despite her frustration with me, she still hadn't taken hers off.

"There's no way those are jewels," she said. "They're just pieces of dull glass. Nothing special."

I frowned and swallowed my hurt. *How could she say they were nothing special?*

"Look, after we've grilled Marie about the

ancient power, we're going to have to up your fencing game," Cass said. "You can't have Marie beat you. Fencing requires the physical agility of ballet, the strength of—" She was about to launch into an explanation when Dahlia appeared.

"Hi!" I said, greeting her with gusto. She was a breath of fresh air after Cass's remark.

"I'm so happy to be here," she said with a wide smile. "Are you ready to talk? We need to go somewhere a little more private, right?"

"What?" Cass asked, her hands on her hips. "Excuse me, Dahlia, but you're not supposed to be here."

"Cass, Dahlia is here to help us prepare for the Hidden Moon Festival," I said. "I really want her to participate. It's where her parents met and fell in love. Plus, she's a great artist. We need some help with those backdrops!"

"This really is a dream come true for me." Dahlia beamed.

"No, no. The castle painters will finish them in time. They always do. And this goes against protocol." Cass eyed me. If anyone was committed to her duty, it was Cass. How could I convince her not to worry about Dahlia? "You can't just invite *anybody* to be a part of the castle festivities, Raps."

"She's my top choice for the artists' assistant," I said, ushering Dahlia aside. Cass shook her head and began sharpening the swords. I lowered my voice to speak to Dahlia. "So, I'm actually making a secret present for Cassandra that I'll give to her during the festival. And I want it to be something really beautiful—about friendship. I'm going to need your best, most colorful paints."

"That won't be a problem," Dahlia said. "I promise I'll get you everything you need." She took a deep breath. "Can I just say it's amazing to be here right now? Getting ready for the festival, behind the scenes. Ooh, I just love it! Do you really need help with those backdrops?"

"I think we have it covered, but maybe you should make it look as though you're taking notes?" I asked. "It'll keep Cass off the scent."

"Sure! I'll walk around like I'm getting a sense of the space," Dahlia said, pulling out her sketchbook and strolling the perimeter.

I walked back over to join Cass. "And why, exactly, do you trust her?" Cass asked when Dahlia was out of earshot.

"Trust me," I said. "She's fine. She's loved this festival ever since she was a little girl. And she's a real artist."

"We don't know her," Cass said. I watched Dahlia sketch the hall. There was nothing off about her. I was sure of it.

"Hello, ladies, are you ready to practice?" It was Marie, who appeared to have not one, but two fencing outfits. This one had a bow on the face mask.

"Yes," I said.

"Before we start, however," Cass said, "we want to know why you've been taking books on Coronan history out of the library. What exactly are you after?"

"You are most brash," Marie said.

"And you're suspicious," Cass countered.

Dahlia took several steps in our direction to sketch the stage from a different perspective.

"I was hoping to embroider my fencing outfit with historical emblems of the kingdom, if you must know," Marie said, tears welling in her eyes. "It was going to be a surprise."

"Do you need any colorful thread?" Dahlia asked. "I have some really beautiful spools all the way from East Tal."

"Hervanian thread is the finest in the world." Marie's brow crinkled with offense. "Why would I ever use anything else?" She sniffed.

"Uh, sorry," Dahlia replied.

"I'd love to see the thread," I said to Dahlia. "And thank you for researching our emblems, Marie. That's really thoughtful." I handed Marie a tissue. The Hervanian princess was appearing more and more to be innocent.

Cass grunted in frustration. "We'll get back to this, Marie. But right now I'm not sure the premises are safe. If you'll excuse me, I need to escort someone out of the castle." Cass nodded at Dahlia.

I was really making her job difficult, but I had to believe she would understand when she saw my gift.

"Don't worry, I'll show her the door," I said, gesturing for Dahlia to follow me. "I'll talk to you later," I whispered as we headed to the exit. "Tomorrow."

"Absolutely," Dahlia whispered in return. And then she left.

Cass glared at me.

"She's gone," I said.

"In my culture, ladies-in-waiting must display obedience!" Marie exclaimed.

"Not here," I said, meeting Cass's exasperated eyes. "Not here."

25
CASSANDRA

"**Y**ou can't invite people into the castle until you get to know them better," I explained to Raps as she sketched out her vision for the backdrop of the great hall. We'd had a particularly exhausting fencing practice. Marie was energized by her anger at me. "Especially not now, when the book has gone missing."

"But Dahlia gave me no reason not to trust her." She looked up from her drawing. "Do you really think that my instincts are so wrong?"

"I think they're *untrained* instincts," I replied.

"Isn't that what instincts are?" she asked.

"Not when it comes to security."

There was a knock on the door.

"I'll get it," I said. "Who is it?"

"A special delivery for the princess," a man said as Rapunzel hopped off her bed to join me. I gestured for her to stay back. I was still her lady-in-waiting, after all, and it was my job to answer the door. Marco stood at the threshold with three books: *Old Saporian: A Guide*; the Saporian dictionary; and *Fairy Tales of Saporia*.

"Thank you so much," I said.

"Yes, we can't wait to read them," Rapunzel said.

We reached for them at the same time, and the spearhead fell from my pocket. I bent down to retrieve it as quickly as possible.

"What's that?" Marco asked.

"Lucky rock," I answered.

"May I see it? I'm always interested in old rocks. They're like old words, aren't they? Carrying history in their shape," Marco said.

"No," I said. "Lucky rock."

"She is so superstitious," Rapunzel said, stepping in front of me. "If anyone else touches her lucky rock she thinks it will lose its luck."

"I see," said Marco. "No problem, though you certainly didn't strike me as the fanciful type."

"You don't know me very well," I said.

"I guess I'll be on my way then," Marco said. "Here's a note from Xavier."

As soon as Marco was gone, Rapunzel opened the small envelope. It seemed impossible that Xavier's big hands could have formed such small letters. The writing was tiny and precise.

"What's it say?" I asked.

"'Where two languages meet, a third forms between them. The place in between two souls, a place that wouldn't exist without what each one brings to it. Enjoy the art of translation!'"

"Huh?"

"I think he means that languages are kind of like colors. Each stands on its own, but when they meet, they create something new," she said.

"I don't get it," I said.

As Rapunzel copied the words in her diary, I opened the Saporian dictionary, focusing on the title of the poem that followed "The Lost Lagoon": "Lunnatee."

"It means 'having to do with the moon,'" I said.

"What does?" Rapunzel asked, looking up.

"'Lunnatee,' the next poem," I said.

"Oh, oh!" Rapunzel said. She clapped her hands, unable to contain her enthusiasm. "We need to go there when the moon is bright!"

CHAPTER TWENTY-FIVE

"It's true that we've never been to the lagoon in the night," I said. "This has to be a clue."

"But the last time we snuck out at night . . ." she said.

She didn't need to complete the sentence. "I'm willing to take the risk if you are," I said.

She paused, touching her hair.

"This is about Corona," I said.

She nodded solemnly. "And no one will ever know," she said, as if she could read my mind.

"Tomorrow," I said.

"Why not tonight?" she asked.

"We need to interview the chefs for the cooking demonstrations. And after that, we're evaluating the tailors. We can't appear as though anything is out of the ordinary. And anyway, it's cloudy tonight. We need the light of the moon to be as clear as possible."

"But do we have time?" she asked, her eyes brimming with emotion. "You're only staying for another five days. Unless . . . you've changed your mind?"

"No," I said. "I haven't. A lot can happen in five days. It's plenty of time."

"If you say so," she said, burying her face in the book.

"I say so," I said.

26

RAPUNZEL

The next day, the sights and sounds of the marketplace were a pleasing jolt to the senses. I pulled my cloak over my shoulders and around my face, delighted to be an anonymous shopper on a bustling afternoon. Cassandra was at a meeting for all the castle staff in preparation for the festival. With my hair as a helper, I was able to descend from my window without anyone even noticing I'd slipped away. If I hurried, I would only be gone for an hour.

For the briefest moment, I was free, and as I took in the scene around me, my heart jumped inside my chest. Nearby, a spice seller touted an orange powder that she swore would enliven any stew. And when I leaned over to sniff it, it made my eyes water. We shared a laugh, and she presented me with bunches of rosemary, marjoram, and sage. I closed my eyes and inhaled their scents. We had these spices in the castle garden, of course, but there was something about seeing them displayed on the seller's cart that made them seem new.

The baker with the sweet blackberry-and-cream pastries was open, as well, and I made sure to stop by her little shop. The aroma of almost-burning butter lured me toward the small shop like an invisible rope. A bell above the door rang as I entered.

"Why a cloak on so warm a day, dear?" the baker asked. Her cheeks were pink and her face appeared even more round because of the bonnet on her head.

"Protection from the sun," I said. "I'm very fair." A small film of perspiration had gathered on my brow, and I dabbed it with a handkerchief.

"What are these?" I asked, pointing to the buns that Cassandra had bought for us the other day.

"Blackberry buns," she said.

"These are my favorite treats," I said. "What's in them?"

"That's my secret," she said, giving me a jolly grin.

I couldn't even wait to get out of the shop before I devoured one, and she laughed as she watched me.

Now it was time to get down to business—the reason I went that day, and without Cass.

I knew how much Cass liked going to the market, and that she would be upset if she knew I went without her, but this needed to be a solo trip. First of all, it was nice to have a little break from Cass, who could be downright paranoid about safety.

I also wanted more time alone with Dahlia to discuss Cass's gift. I'd decided the night before that it had to be a small painting, and only for Cassandra's eyes. But I needed some supplies.

Dahlia's cart was decorated with the most extraordinarily rich colors: deep blues and bright oranges, teal and maroon, jewel tones; the array of paints was wider than any I'd ever seen.

"Hi! I was going to come by later to help you paint . . ." Dahlia said. Freckles dotted her nose. Her eyes were green and the dress she wore, which was an eggplant color, set them off like gems.

"Yes, but I wanted to make sure I caught you alone for my secret project. Can you show me your latest shipment of colors?" I asked.

"A boat arrived at dawn with new shades from

CHAPTER TWENTY-SIX

Skaron. They have the best paint in all the world."

"Wow," I said as she opened a drawer and displayed over one hundred colors. "I can't even explain what I'm feeling right now. The possibilities for expression are exploding in my mind."

"Rapunzel, you are a real artist, aren't you?" she asked.

"Yes," I said. And it felt good to say it. Finally, someone who really wanted to talk about the same things I did!

"Painting is my favorite," Dahlia said. "Though I draw, too. Would you like to see my pastels?"

"I'd love to," I said.

She was revealing a tray of gorgeous colors when I felt a tap on my shoulder.

"Rapunzel?" I turned around to see Cassandra. "What are you doing here?"

"Just picking out some paint for the festival," I said. Why did I feel like I was getting in trouble?

"I really need to get her back to the castle," Cassandra said to Dahlia. Turning to me, she said, "You're not supposed to be out without me. Or a guard."

"She just wanted some paint," Dahlia said. "What's the crime in that? Princess, would you like me to bring these paints back to the castle later?"

"I'd love that," I said. "Can you come right to my room?"

"Yes!" Dahlia said.

"Rapunzel's busy," Cass said, ushering me away. "She has to prepare for a fencing match in front of the entire kingdom. She'll be meeting vendors, attending lectures, and being an all-around representative of the royal family. She's not going to have time to mingle with one person for more than a few minutes."

Dahlia pulled back and shot me a quizzical look. *It's fine*, I mouthed. "I'll see you then!"

Dahlia smiled hopefully at me.

"We need to get you home," Cassandra said, ushering me away. "Have you lost your mind? You could be confined even more if your parents knew you were out at the market without me. And inviting someone back to your personal room? That breaks every rule there is."

"I'm fine," I assured her. If only she knew that I was there for her, to buy the tools to create a painting that would convince her to stay in Corona, where she belonged.

Later that evening, after I'd interviewed the national bocce team and tested out the court for smoothness and levelness with the team captain, and then met with the crocheting league and admired their elaborate and delicate blankets, Cass and I returned to my room.

"Did you leave the door open?" Cass asked me as she pushed it open.

"Gosh, no," I said.

"That's weird," Cass said. "Because when I was trying to unlock it, I actually locked it, which means it was unlocked."

"I always lock the door. Besides, weren't you the last one in here, when you fetched my fencing gear?" I asked. "Did *you* forget?"

"Please," she said as she struck a match. "Such a grievous lapse in protocol would never—"

She lit the central lantern. We both gasped.

The bookshelves had been torn apart—books were everywhere. The door to my wardrobe was open, gowns scattered on the floor. The sofa cushions were overturned. My personal drawers had been pulled out from my bureau, all of my collections and papers having been rifled through.

I plunged my hand beneath my mattress, where my diary remained intact, safe.

Thank goodness, I thought as tears rolled down my cheeks.

27

CASSANDRA

The intruder hadn't actually taken anything, and that made it all the more unnerving.

Rapunzel and I walked to the lagoon that night. We had decided that despite the break-in— or rather, because of it—we had to go to the lagoon as we'd planned.

I would never show it, but I was rattled. Someone had dared break into the princess's room? What kind of a brazen fool would do such a thing? And where had the guards been? Playing cards? Taking a nap? Gossiping? It was a good thing I was getting out of there—where the standards had slipped. And yet my stomach churned. Clearly they needed me more than ever. I was the only person in the place who could do the job properly.

Or was I?

This had happened under my watch. I clutched my side, where a pain had formed.

Where had I gone wrong?

After we'd cleaned up Rapunzel's room, we'd done everything according to our routine. In addition to the Hidden Moon Festival duties, we'd dined with her parents and the Hervanians. Marie was still sore with me, but I didn't believe this was her work. Someone as fastidious as she wouldn't have left that kind of mess. Raps had an evening walk with Eugene and a fireside chat with the queen before lights out. During that time, I'd been preparing for the festival, checking in with all of the maids and making sure they understood their duties.

I didn't want to alert the guards about the break-in—that would have been a disaster. My father would have stepped in, and I didn't want to risk him finding out about the lagoon. But the break-in had definitely made our quest more pressing. Whoever had broken in was on a search, and I had a terrible feeling someone else was looking for the ancient power. Why else would her jewelry box not have been raided? Any thief worth his salt would know its contents were worth a fortune. That wasn't the fortune this intruder was after.

At half past ten, Raps and I tiptoed down a back staircase, through the kitchen, and out of the larder window. From there we made a mad dash to the lagoon. Now, as we walked through the forest that had become so familiar to us, I tried to let Rapunzel know how cautious she needed to be around strangers.

"I think it was Dahlia," I said.

"What? Why in the world would it be Dahlia?" she said.

"There's something sneaky about her. It wouldn't surprise me if she had a secret desire to take over the kingdom," I said.

"What? I'm telling you, you have her all wrong," Raps said. "Kinnaird said that LaFleur was examining regional geography. . . ."

"He's writing a ballet!" I said. I was done with LaFleur as a suspect. It had to be someone fresh— someone I didn't know much about. Who was the most recent addition to our lives? Who had wormed her way into Raps's heart? Dahlia. Plus, she'd overheard us talking about the ancient power. I pushed aside some branches as the familiar gulch came into view. "If I'm not going to be here to protect you, you can't go around inviting people into your chambers! For all you know, you could be inviting an enemy of the state right into the heart of the castle! Is that what you want?"

"What I want is to have friends," she said. To my surprise, she took a gentle but firm hold of my arm. "You're starting to sound like my parents."

"That's ridiculous."

"Not everyone is trying to hurt me, Cass. Or you."

"Except that someone broke into your room!" I said, more sharply than I'd intended to. "You trust everyone, and that's not appropriate!"

"And you trust no one," she said, crossing her arms. "Not Dahlia, not Eugene. Not even me . . . anymore."

"I trust Owl. And Fidella and Maximus. And even Pascal. There. That's four . . . beings."

"Maybe it was a common thief," she suggested.

"Who didn't want your jewels?" I replied.

"I trust her, so please give Dahlia a chance! She's so creative and a fellow artist. You never want to talk about artsy stuff with me," she said.

"That's not true," I said. "I mean, I guess I get a little skeptical when you start talking about see-ing people's auras and the feeling that green gives you, or how something is so white it practically has a sound. . . ."

"But sometimes I need to talk about those things, just like you want to talk about armor or spearheads," she said.

"But that stuff is interesting," I said.

"Humph," Raps said.

"Double humph," I said.

"Ugh! Cass! So can you open your mind . . . just a little?" Rapunzel asked.

"No," I said.

"It wasn't Dahlia," she said. "I'm not going to bend on this. I just know it. In my gut."

"Okay, okay. I'll believe you," I said.

"Really?" she asked, delighted.

"Yeah, fine. Talk with her during the Hidden Moon Festival. But don't take her beyond the public areas."

"Thank you," Rapunzel said. We faced each other, appearing to have some kind of staring contest. "Are we going to do this, or what?"

"Oh, there's no way I'm not doing this," I said.

Now that Rapunzel's hair was long, we could travel over the gulch in no time. Rapunzel tossed her hair across the chasm and wound it around a tree branch. Usually, she let me hang on her back so we could leap together. But tonight, while she flew over the cragged rocks to the lagoon, she left me on the other side to navigate the area by myself.

"Thanks a lot," I muttered under my breath.

"Wow," I heard her say from the other side as I struggled across the awkward passage.

"What?" I asked, wiping sweat from my brow. The moon was at its zenith, shining brightly from the very top of the sky. Cool water rushed under my feet. "Are there jewels? Weapons? What do you see?"

"It's just so beautiful," Rapunzel said. "I think the lagoon has a tide just like the ocean. The water's higher."

"But what do you see?" I asked again, trudging through the gulch. "Are there jewels or not?"

"I can't tell!" she called back.

When I arrived on the other side, Rapunzel had her skirts gathered in her hands and was knee-deep in the lagoon, staring into the water as if in a trance.

"Cass, look!" She pointed to a school of fish as bright as drops of sunlight. "I've heard of fish that change color at night, but I've never seen them."

"Whoa!" I said as they circled the jewels, which

now also appeared to be a shimmering yellow.

"Have you ever seen anything like it?" Rapunzel said.

"The jewels must have some secret power at midnight," I said. "We have to get them."

"Except my hair," she said. "I can't risk getting it wet."

She was right. Queen Arianna would not be pleased if Raps showed up with a dripping head of hair. It wasn't easy to dry seventy feet of unbreakable locks—it took hours of laying it out in direct sunlight. Rapunzel and I had made up a million reasons why she needed frequent hair washes to cover for other outings to the lagoon, but we had always come in the morning, when we'd had time for those cover-ups. We didn't have time for that now, and there was no way her hair would dry on its own.

"I'll go get them," I said.

While Rapunzel waited on the rocks, I dove for the sparkling gems, but what I came up with instead was the same stones we'd known about for months. It was all just a trick of the light.

"So much for the great art of translation," I said. "We're not any closer to figuring out this poem."

"What are we missing?" Rapunzel asked. "We have to be missing something. That water looks too magical to be just . . . water."

"It's pretty great in here," I said, splashing around.

"Don't rub it in!" Rapunzel said.

"Sorry," I said, and then splashed her.

"Oh!" she said, and splashed me back.

"Do you think I'll change color, too, if I swim with those fish?" I said. It was fun to tease her. "I'll just swim to the waterfall and back and then we can head back to the castle."

"Fine," said Rapunzel, her arms crossed.

I dove under the water and swam for as long as I could while holding my breath. My goal was to make it to the waterfall without having to come up for air, and I was almost there. When I surfaced, about to tip my head under the rushing water, I screamed in surprise.

Rapunzel's face peered through the other side of the waterfall.

"Ah!" I said.

"I gotcha!" she said. She grabbed me under my arms.

"Ahhh!" I said again as she used her hair to gain

momentum and swung us both around the tree branch, then way up in the air. At what felt like the moon's zenith, she let go.

We looked at each other in midair and, screaming with laughter, plunged into the lagoon.

"Water fight!" I said, giggling as I surfaced.

"Are you sure about that?" she asked, her eyes sparkling with mischief. She grabbed her hair, which was dripping like a whale's tail.

"Um, actually . . ." I started.

"Too late!" she said joyfully, and shaking her head, she flung her sopping wet hair over the lagoon, creating a mini rainstorm.

"No fair," I said, wiping water from my eyes. "Hey—if we push those rocks together, do you think we could make a waterslide, like over the waterfall?

"Only one way to find out," Rapunzel said.

Back at the castle, we came up with a few creative solutions to dry Rapunzel's hair as quickly and quietly as possible. First we used every towel we could find to wring out as much as we could—but it wasn't enough. Then we hung her hair out the window and hoped for a strong breeze.

"We're going to have to create our own breeze!"

CHAPTER TWENTY-SEVEN

Raps said, her cheek resting on the windowsill.

I called for Owl, who gathered the other owls. They flapped their wings and sailed Raps's hair through the air until it was nearly dry.

"This is kind of weird," Raps said.

"I think we need more time to figure things out," I said.

"Really?" Raps asked. "Why? You've changed your mind?"

"No," I said firmly. "It's just that there have been two security breaches lately—the stolen book and the break-in."

One of the guiding principles of the guard said: *Where there's a need for soldiers, we arise, prepared and ready to face battle.* Who was I if I left in the middle of this chaos? And as for this mystery, we were close. I could feel it with every fiber of my being.

"You know we can find the lagoon's ancient power together," she said, as though she could read my mind. Then a shadow crossed her face. "But the festival is tomorrow. . . ."

"So we'll go back to the lagoon tomorrow night after the festival is over," I said. "I'll bring my maps; you get out the dictionaries. We'll translate every word of this poem and get to the bottom of this. Then I'll have fulfilled my every obligation to Corona."

"That sounds perfect," Rapunzel said as the owls continued to dry her hair. "Wait—except, tomorrow's the eclipse. And there needs to be moonlight, according to the poem. . . ."

"Oh, right. . . . I guess it'll have to be the next night then."

Raps looked hopeful. "You're going to stay an extra day?"

"Just one," I said, sounding more sure than I felt.

"Okay. This is going to be fun," she said, flashing her brightest smile as the owls continued their swoops and dives.

28

RAPUNZEL

On the dawn of the festival, everyone wore white to represent the moon that would be absent that night, just as Dahlia had described. With docents guiding the villagers into position, the crowd formed a crescent shape.

Marie and I stood on the balcony in our fencing gear, taking in the masses of people. True to her word, her suit was embroidered with historical symbols of Corona. Her needlework was as exact as her battle-tackle. I had to admit, my opponent was dressed for success. My own suit had a giant sun emblem on it. I touched it with my fist and waved to the crowd. They cheered for both of us. Then

Marie began her usual set of stretches and martial arts moves. I took some deep, focusing breaths.

Cass straightened my mask as she gave me a pep talk. "Remember," she said, "fencing is mental as much as it is physical. Stay focused."

"Got it. And what about the hair?" I asked. "Is it off-limits?"

"For sword grabbing, yes, but as far as a distraction technique . . . Well, I don't see a problem there."

"Could be fun," I said. "Marie is always up for a challenge."

"Wait a second, what is he doing?" Cass asked, pointing to LaFleur, who with his team of dancers was passing candles out to the crowd. He stood out in his white robe trimmed with bright gold. He also wore an elaborate headpiece with streamers flowing from it.

"Looks like he's trying to add some atmosphere?" I said as the small lights seemed to multiply.

"Or starting a fire!" Cass said. "And of course the fire regulator is nowhere in sight. Ugh! I'm going to have to get down there and keep an eye on things. After that I'll be refereeing the bocce game, and then acting as a royal taster for the great bake-off."

"I bet there'll be so many amazing desserts," I

said. "Apple tarts and chocolate cakes, pastries and meringues, tortes and—"

"Yeah, well, I'd rather be leading a weapons demonstration," Cass said, tightening my belt. "But they've assigned that to the guards. Good luck! I'm not taking my eyes off LaFleur until every one of those candles is extinguished. Otherwise twinkle toes down there is going to turn us all into soot."

"Hello," my mother called to the people as she and my father joined Marie and I on the balcony. "And welcome to the first event of the Hidden Moon Festival!" The crowd cheered. "We are delighted and honored to have Lady Marie of Hervan joining our dear princess, Rapunzel, in a friendly fencing match to kick off the festivities." Once again applause washed over us like a wave. My fingers began to tingle with nervousness and excitement. "Are you ready, girls?"

"I am," I said with a smile.

"Always," Marie said. Her fierceness still surprised me.

"*Prêtes . . . Allez!*" Dad shouted.

We parried and counter parried and before long, Marie had pulled a feint and scored a point.

The audience cheered at Marie's victory and then chanted my name. It was a friendly match, of course, but people couldn't seem to help reveling in the entertainment of it all. Marie assumed a ready stance as I regained my composure. I could hear Cass in my mind, telling me to focus and strategize. As she'd said, fencing was as mental as it was physical.

"Find your foe's mental weakness," Cass had instructed. "This is the key."

My breath was loud and rhythmic under the cover of my face mask. *Pride,* I thought as I met Marie's gaze. *Her weakness is pride.*

Before I could register any more thoughts, Marie lunged and scored another point. Out of the corner of my eye, I saw my mother's concerned expression.

This is part of the plan, I thought, faking a move, which Marie quickly reversed, scoring yet again. The villagers were quiet. I imagined they didn't want to see their princess so handily defeated. Marie's eyes were smiling. Her confidence was up. Now was the time!

I spun away from her, causing my braid to create a whirling shield around me. With a balestra and a low lunge, I attacked and scored a point of my own. The crowd cheered. Marie grinned. This was a match!

CHAPTER TWENTY-EIGHT

. . .

"Okay, so more about my special project," I started telling Dahlia after the fencing competition. Marie and I had battled it out with our whole hearts. In the end, it was a tie. We were both okay with that. "You have shown yourself to be a most worthy competitor," Marie had said with a bow. "You're the best guest," I'd replied, "because you challenge us to rise to the occasion." She'd beamed.

Now Dahlia and I were in the grand hall, putting finishing touches on the backdrop for the banquet, and I was whispering because I didn't want anyone to hear me. I knew that part of the power of my gift to Cassandra would be the surprise of it all, so I didn't want anyone to overhear my plan.

"Can you speak up?" Dahlia asked over the din. "I can't really hear you."

"I want to make something really unusual," I whispered, waving to passersby.

"Is there any way we could go somewhere a little quieter?" Dahlia asked.

"Sure," I said, though Cass's words about not letting her beyond the spaces that had been made public were circling in my mind. "Follow me."

We went to the library, but it was packed. Kinnaird was entertaining the children—and a beaming Eugene—with tales of Flynn Rider.

We tried the royal dining room, but the chefs in there were so busy demonstrating broth-making techniques to eager home cooks that I could tell we were underfoot.

We tried the wardrobe room, but the royal dressmakers were lecturing about the latest sewing methods to a crowd of tailors.

We even went to the gardens, but the grounds-keepers and gardeners were leading educational tours.

"Just come to my room," I said. I had some time before my next event and the ball was still a couple of hours away. Thankfully, the guards were so distracted by all the activities in the castle that I was able to sneak Dahlia up a back staircase unnoticed.

I knew Cassandra wouldn't be pleased, but I really thought she was overreacting. Nothing about Dahlia seemed dangerous. She was simply a fellow artist, not an enemy of the state. Cass was looking on the dark side, as usual.

"So this is what a princess's room looks like!" Dahlia said, taking in the high ceilings, the huge windows framed by flowing drapes, and my enormous bed.

"Yes," I said. "This is my room."

As Dahlia ran her hands along the intricate tiles around my fireplace, admiring the design, I knew I'd been right all along. All she cared about was art. "Tell me more about this project," Dahlia said, her dimples deepening with her smile.

"Well," I said, making myself comfortable on a floor cushion, "I want to make something really special." Things had been going so well with Cass lately. The perfect gift might be all she needed to convince her to stay. It was weird, but I felt like I could speak to Dahlia about my artistic thoughts without any embarrassment. Cassandra would've probably made fun of me, but Dahlia was nodding in genuine understanding. I gestured to a matching cushion as Pascal lit the fireplace.

"What's your vision?" Dahlia asked, crossing her legs, cupping her chin in her hand, and leaning in.

"The scene is a gorgeous . . ." I paused. I had promised not to tell anyone about the lagoon, so I tried to make it sound theoretical. I tried to come up with a synonym for lagoon and thought of Marco's word. "Sinkhole."

"A sinkhole," Dahlia said, contemplating the word. Her face was illuminated in a pinkish light by the fire. "An ugly word for a possibly beautiful place. I like it. I have a thing for contradictions."

"I want to paint the morning light at the sink-hole. And I want it to feel magical," I said. "The color should be ethereal."

"Mmmm," Dahlia said. "I'm feeling purples. I'm feeling smooth textures."

"Yes," I said. "But this is just the background."

"Go on."

"The foreground will be the portrait of me and Cassandra," I said.

"Are you sure?" she asked, furrowing her brow.

"She's not what you think," I said. "She's the most amazing person I've ever met."

"Really?" Dahlia asked with genuine curiosity.

"She's funny and strong and so, so smart," I said as Dahlia smiled and nodded. Her open-mindedness was refreshing.

"Let's get started," Dahlia said.

She stood up and opened her suitcase, which was full of her imported paints. She must have had at least two hundred colors and twenty different brushes. "Are you interested at all in pen and ink?" She opened yet another case holding pens of varying thickness and wells of fine black ink. The creative possibilities were endless.

"I love these," I said, picking up one of the pens.

"I'm so into pen and ink right now, too," she said.

CHAPTER TWENTY-EIGHT

"And I want this painting to be small." I held up my hands to demonstrate.

"Why?" Dahlia asked, her head tilted with curiosity.

"People always think that bigger is better, but sometimes the most precious items are small, because they're private," I said. This was all true. But the main reason that I wanted the painting to be small and light was so it could fit inside of a drawer, where it could be hidden away so no one would ever guess we had been to the lagoon. Of course, I also wanted it to be small enough to fit inside Cassandra's satchel in case she still decided to leave. "This piece needs to be portable."

"I love that," Dahlia said, her face lighting up. "I actually just got chills. Art hangs on walls, but why shouldn't it be carried? We need art with us all the time. At least, I do." I smiled. "I brought some wood to make a frame," she continued. "And canvas, of course. Show me again how big you think it should be?"

I brought out my diary and held it up. "About this size."

"Is that a journal?" Dahlia asked. I nodded. She ran her hands over it. "It's *stunning*."

"Thanks." I'd put a lot of thought into making it

mine with a few designs. It felt good to be appreciated.

"May I hold it?" she asked.

"Yes, but I'd rather you not look inside," I said.

"Never," Dahlia said, admiring the flourishes I'd added to the cover to make it mine. "I just wanted to feel it. These touches you've added are so creative. They feel very . . . you."

"Thanks," I said, amazed that someone who barely knew me could recognize that. "Wait, what if we made two canvases, hinged together, that closed like a book?"

"Like a locket?" Dahlia asked, her eyes growing wide.

"Uh-huh," I said. "We could finish the outside of it, so it would appear to be a book, but it would really be a double painting!"

"Genius!" Dahlia said. "Let me just see what hardware I have. I bet I have a clasp that will work as a binding. I also make jewelry, you know."

"You do?" I asked. She nodded as she searched in a pocket of her bag. "I really want to learn more about that. I made this bracelet I'm wearing."

I showed her the lagoon stone in the piece of leather wrapped around my wrist.

"Let me see?" she said. I extended my hand. "Can I hold it?"

CHAPTER TWENTY-EIGHT

"Sorry, I, um, don't really like to take it off."

"Why not?" she asked, her inquisitive eyes meeting my own in a mini challenge.

Cassandra and I had never outright said that we wouldn't take our bracelets off, but ever since I'd made them, neither one of us had. It was as much a part of my arm as the small freckle at the base of my thumb, or the veins that crisscrossed under the pale skin of my wrist.

"I just want to see how it's made," Dahlia said. "I would never take it. I'm impressed that you created this yourself. I'd think that as a princess you have all the jewelry you'd ever want, right?"

"Yes, but I like to make things," I said.

"Me too," Dahlia said. "It's pretty much what makes me . . . me. And you picked such an unusual stone. Where did you find it?"

"By the beach," I said. That wasn't a lie. It was just that it was by the beach of the lagoon, not the ocean.

"If you want, I can also teach you some advanced jewelry-making techniques," she said.

"You know what? I'm being silly. I can take it off," I said, and untied the leather knot. "Here."

29

CASSANDRA

Maybe I don't have to leave, I thought as I wandered through the quiet marketplace after refereeing the bocce tournament. I'd been sent there for sugar because the chefs had run out of it and the supply had to be replenished before the bake-off. Most of the vendors were at the Hidden Moon Festival, and it was peaceful. Seeing all the different shops and stalls, I was reminded of why I loved this place so much. I looked around for that annoying painter, but I didn't see her. I guess she'd gone to the festival to help Raps after all. I didn't trust that girl, but as long as they stayed in the public eye, there wasn't much harm she could do.

I thought more about my options. If I stayed in Corona I would become captain of the guard. Rapunzel would place me in the position, without a doubt. If I went somewhere else, I'd be an outsider. People don't like outsiders. *I* don't. It could take a long time for me to find a guard position, if I found one at all. At least here I was in with the future queen.

And Raps was going to be a good queen, even though she didn't quite believe it yet. She took control when she needed to. She didn't make me feel weird about not knowing how to swim. And she *was* loyal . . . except for the part when she'd told Eugene about our night out. But he'd been silent. Maybe that was part of being under the love spell—you just did what the other person said when it came to stuff like that. She definitely hadn't said anything about the lagoon to him. I was on the lookout for any knowledge he might have. The kid was an open book. It was clear he knew nothing.

Plus, Raps and I were a good team. I'd been the one to discover the three trees. But she had been the one to unearth the ancient poem that clued me in about the lagoon. I had done the groundwork, but she had given the work a purpose by connecting it to Corona's oldest and greatest power. I had led her to the lagoon, but she had gotten me past my fear of the water. I had shown her freedom, and she had taught me how to swim.

That was the thing. The captain of the guard and the royal family needed that level of cooperation. They had to work together to keep the people safe and happy.

In the midst of my thoughts, I bumped right into the bakery. My stomach growled as the bakery smell wafted toward me. Blackberry rolls!

I decided I should get some for Rapunzel. She loved those things.

"May I help you, dear?" the baker asked.

"Yeah. I'll take fifteen bags of sugar for the castle and two blackberry rolls to go." I handed her some coins.

"These have become quite popular lately," she said. "Ever since the princess declared them her favorite, I can't make them fast enough! Isn't she a lovely soul?"

"She's pretty great."

She smiled at me and placed two steaming buns in my basket, promising to deliver the sugar to the castle posthaste. I quickly covered the buns with a linen cloth, hoping they would still be warm when I reached Rapunzel, then headed back toward the castle.

"Cassandra?" someone called.

"Yes?" I said, turning to see Xavier at his blacksmith stall.

"Are you on your way to the castle?" he asked.

"I am," I answered.

"I have something for Rapunzel," he said, handing me a book. It was a tattered volume, *The Lost Language: Insights into Saporian Myths and Legends*, with a leather bookmark placed among its pages. "I found this book last night on Marco's desk. He must have left it behind by accident. Will you bring it to her?"

"Definitely," I said. This could hold the answers we were looking for! I was dying to open it up, but it would be so much more fun to do so with Rapunzel, to make the discovery together.

"Thank you so much, Xavier," I said. "I'm sure this will quell the princess's voracious appetite for literature."

As soon as I was out of sight, I broke into a run. I was so excited to share the book with her. I was almost out of breath when I arrived at her door. I didn't even bother to knock. I ran inside.

"Rapunzel!" I said.

She was sitting on a cushion, and Dahlia was there, with Rapunzel's bracelet in her hand.

"Cass, you're not supposed to be here until later," Raps said.

"Does my advice mean nothing to you?" I asked her. She blanched.

"Hi," Dahlia said. "We're having a private art session. So if you wouldn't mind . . . ?" She was gesturing with her hand, flinging Raps's bracelet around as she did.

"I do mind," I said. "I am Rapunzel's lady-in-waiting. What are you doing here?"

"We're making art. Are those blackberry buns I smell?" Dahlia asked.

I ignored her. "It's my job to protect you, Rapunzel. You can't just have people in your room! What if something had happened to you? It'd be all my fault."

"It's Dahlia," Rapunzel said. "She's fine—just an artist, like me."

"I wouldn't hurt anyone," Dahlia said, the bracelet dangling from her hand. "Maybe you need to make some art so that you can relax."

"Relax? This is a princess," I said, pointing to

CHAPTER TWENTY-NINE

Rapunzel. "This person is the beating heart of this entire kingdom."

Though I couldn't pretend it was *just* that. I'd told Rapunzel not to trust Dahlia, and here they were *in her room.*

"Cass?" she said, gently taking the bracelet from Dahlia's hand. Could she have thought I didn't see it? "I think you're overreacting. It was too noisy around the castle for us to have a real conversation, and I have this special project . . ."

"Stop!" I said. "You need to stop thinking of yourself as a girl with some kind of artistic dream and realize that your future has been determined."

"Cass?" she said again, this time in a more pleading tone.

"You are the future queen," I said. "And it's time you started acting like one."

Hurt flashed across her face like lightning. I continued anyway. "I have my destiny, as well. But it's not here. And it's not with you."

"Whoa," Dahlia said.

"What exactly are you saying, Cass?" Rapunzel asked.

"I'm saying that I'm done," I said. "I'm finally leaving."

30
RAPUNZEL

The look in Cassandra's eyes was as fierce as a tiger's. Her mouth was drawn tight with hurt: a straight line, lips white with pressure.

"You're leaving *now*?" I asked, leaping up and reaching for her hand. "But the festival isn't over. We still have the ball!"

"Where are you going?" Dahlia asked.

"It's none of your concern," Cassandra said.

"Um, maybe it would be best if you were on your way, Dahlia," I said as gently as possible.

"No, she needs to wait until after the festival. They can't know that you have a stranger in your room," Cassandra said. "You should know that by now. And yes, I'm really leaving. Did you think I was going to stay?"

My heart sank like a stone, and for a moment I felt like a total fool. Tears stung my eyes. "We've been having so much fun together. And yesterday was perfect because . . . I knew what it was like to have a best friend." Pascal grimaced. "A *human* best friend," I clarified.

I noticed a book under Cassandra's arms, but she didn't seem like she wanted to share it with me. She held it close to her chest.

"Wait, what did you do yesterday?" Dahlia asked. She really didn't seem able to take a hint.

"Nothing," I said as quickly as possible.

I widened my eyes at Cassandra to let her know that I had not told Dahlia anything about the lagoon. That was still our secret. It would remain so until we decided otherwise.

Cassandra cast a quick glance at Dahlia, registering her confused expression.

"Did you do something exciting?" Dahlia asked. Cassandra and I held each other's gaze. "Or . . . not allowed? Ooooh, that's it, isn't it? As an artist, I love to break boundaries, which is just another name for rules, you know. Artists are born to break rules!"

"Great choice of friend to bring back to the castle, Raps," Cassandra said. "Really stellar."

"We went on a simple outing," I said to Dahlia, having a hard time disguising the edge that had climbed into my voice. Dahlia tilted her head at me, assessing if I was telling the truth or not.

"The last few weeks have just been a lark," Cassandra said, ignoring Dahlia. "You can have a life of fun, Rapunzel, but I can't because I'm worried about being banished."

"Why would you be banished?" Dahlia asked. "Though I wouldn't judge you if you were. In stricter countries, artists get banished all the time because of . . ." Cassandra and I both glared at her. "You know, the rule-breaking thing?"

Sensing that Cassandra was on the verge of unsheathing one of her knives, I took a deep breath and said in a calm voice, "Dahlia, Cassandra is being a little dramatic. There's no reason she'd ever be banished. It's, um, a game we like to play sometimes. Who'd get banished first?"

"This is not a game," Cassandra said. "I'm going."

"But what about tomorrow?" I said. "We were going to—"

"The time is now. I knew I'd be able to feel the moment when it arrived. And it's here."

CHAPTER THIRTY

"When you get where you're going, will you at least send word so that if I'm ever queen you can be my captain of the guard?" I asked, wiping tears from my eyes.

"It's not *if* you become queen, Raps, it's when. And that would never work. The queen and the captain of the guard have to have absolute trust in each other."

"Please stay," I said. I couldn't imagine my life in Corona without Cassandra. "Don't you at least want to figure out the—" Aware of Dahlia, I bit my tongue.

"Figure out the what?" Dahlia asked.

"Nothing!" Cassandra and I said at the same time.

"Whoa," Dahlia said. "The energy in here is wild."

"Let me go," Cassandra said. "This is what I need to be happy."

"I guess if this is what you want . . ." I said, struggling to get the words out. "I want you to be happy. But don't you think that you can be happy here?"

"Not when your actions keep putting me in danger," Cassandra said.

"Are you talking about me here?" Dahlia asked. "Because, come on, isn't that just a *tiny* bit of an exaggeration?"

"Your head is in the clouds," Cassandra said, ignoring Dahlia. "And that's a luxury only the barefoot princess can afford. I'm going."

"But—" I started, approaching her with my arms held out.

"Let me go," Cassandra said, stepping backward. "If you want me to be happy, let me go."

"Okay," I said, hands up in surrender. "Okay."

She placed two blackberry buns on my table, in the same spot where I had first served her cookies, and then she left.

My chest felt as narrow and tight as the gulch by the lagoon. Pascal tugged at my dress. He pointed at the door, as if to tell me to go after her.

"But I want her to be happy," I said to him.

"Are you okay?" Dahlia asked. I shook my head. "I don't know if she's the amazing person you think she is. That seemed really dramatic. I mean, I'm an artist—I once wove a dress of corn silk to make a statement about the treatment of silkworms—and even I thought that was over the top!"

I could barely hear her because my heart was thumping so loudly in my ears.

"I'm starving," she said. "Would you mind if I had one of these blackberry rolls?"

"Go right ahead," I said. I had no appetite anyway.

But as she ripped one of them in half, I had to look away.

"You know," Dahlia said with her mouth full, "if you're looking for a new lady-in-waiting, I'm open to it. We could even redecorate. I might suggest some earth tones."

"Dahlia, if you don't mind, I need a little quiet right now," I said. I walked to my window and touched my forehead against the glass. The world outside had never looked so big and empty.

PART THREE

31

CASSANDRA

I dropped the book outside her door. The mystery was hers now. I was out.

I went back to my chambers and started to pack—*again*. Everyone was so busy with the festival I doubted anyone would notice my absence. I'd be out on the road for a fortnight at least. It'd be much quicker on horseback, but I couldn't take a horse. Too obvious. I'd bring what I could carry. I opened my weapons closet. The door creaked a little, as if the furniture knew I was leaving. I ran my hand over the closet's wooden edges, admiring the collection of weapons and tools that I'd amassed over the years and taken care of so diligently. I hated to leave all this behind. Each object had a story—like the day my father had given me his old sword, when I was only eight years old. I remembered how heavy it had been at the time, how my wrist had ached from keeping it upright. Now I could wield it as though it were a feather. And then there was the shot-put ball—the object that had brought Rapunzel and me together.

Why had Raps ignored my advice and allowed Dahlia into her room without anyone there to protect her? Why had she given her the bracelet? I guess Raps trusted anyone, so it was meaningless.

Friends are stupid. That's why I never had any. Just then Owl landed at my window. Owl was the exception. We had an understanding. We knew each other so well without ever having to speak. We didn't need matching bracelets. I looked down at the bracelet around my wrist and thought for a moment about cutting it loose.

Owl nudged me with his beak.

"Okay, fine. I'll keep it on for now. I might need to trade it later." Owl shook his head. "What? Now you're sentimental. How about you just sit and watch, okay?"

I turned back to my weapons closet and chose my sword. Then I selected two knives: one for my belt and one for my boot. I tied my satchel around my waist and grabbed my cloak and lantern. I needed some coins, and I'd have to get some food from the kitchen, though Owl and I could hunt if necessary.

I set out when darkness blanketed the kingdom. Owl hooted, signaling that the coast was clear. I used a vine to reach a tree branch and then shimmied down the trunk. Owl swooped low. I darted beyond the castle wall, silent as a cat. I'd memorized my maps by this point and planned to head south. I'd barely walked through the first field, however, when my foot caught on a root and I twisted my ankle. I nearly cried out in pain. I sucked air through my teeth and gently tried to roll my ankle. It was tender, but not broken.

How could I start out my journey this way? How was I ever going to make it? I hadn't even considered that I would be injured, not with the training I'd done. What a stupid mistake! Owl circled in the indigo night, then came back, settling on a nearby tree. I took a linen cloth from my satchel and wrapped it tightly around my foot. Owl looked at me as if to say this was a bad omen.

"There's no way I'm turning back now," I said,

though my ankle throbbed and indignation burned inside me. Owl blinked. "We'll go to the lagoon for the night."

I knew the way so well I could get there with my eyes shut, and the path was smooth enough that I could make it on my hands and knees. I didn't have a choice. I'd have to spend the night there. If I could hobble through the gulch then I'd be able to get a good night's sleep and soak my foot to reduce the swelling. Owl and I could fish in the morning if we needed to, filling ourselves before we took off for a long day of walking. It was, after all, the only place I knew where no one else would be—at least not in the middle of the night.

I had just reached the mossy part of the path when a hand grabbed me by my arm and yanked me upright. My sword was stolen within a second.

"Take me to the lagoon," a rough voice said.

I struggled, kicking my attacker with my good foot until he buckled behind me. He kept a firm grip on my arm, and as I pulled away, I felt my bracelet snap. I heard Owl's distinctive call as he descended.

32

RAPUNZEL

Several hours passed, and as the sky darkened my mind clouded with worry and doubt. Had I done the right thing by letting her walk away? Should I have fought harder for her to stay? Sounds of the festival drifted up to my room, but I couldn't join in the festivities with such a heavy heart. At last there was a knock on the door. Was it Cass? I wondered. Had she changed her mind? I flew to open the door, but it was Eugene, all dressed up for the ball and holding a bouquet of flowers.

"Gee. Not the reception I was hoping for," he said. "You're not ready?"

"Eugene," I said, and I let myself fall into his arms. He smelled like the citrus shaving soap the royal barbers liked to use on what he called his "sensitive complexion." At first I wasn't sure how I felt about it, but at that moment, the familiar lime scent filled me with comfort as he held me even tighter.

"What happened, Rapunzel?" he asked. "Why are you crying? Come and sit down. Whatever it is, we can fix it together."

"I doubt you can fix this," Dahlia said. "It's girl trouble."

"Well, hi there," Eugene said, noticing Dahlia, who was sketching a picture of Pascal. "I'm Eugene. Who are you?"

"I'm Dahlia," she said, placing her pencil down for a moment. "I've heard so many nice things about you."

"You have?" Eugene asked.

"The townspeople all talk about how kind and gallant you are," Dahlia said.

"Aw, really? That's nice," Eugene said. Dahlia nodded, and then he remembered himself. "But wait, what's going on here?"

"Dahlia is my new friend. She's helping me with

an art project," I explained as I dabbed my eyes. "She came up to my room because we needed some space to work and all the public areas of the castle were crowded because of the festival."

"You know that you really can't have any strangers in your room, right?" Eugene said.

"I know," I said. "But I made my own decision. I saw no harm. I trusted her."

"That counts for a lot," Eugene said. "Though I'm not sure how we'll get her out of here. The castle is still swarmed with guards, making sure that no townspeople—or enemies disguised as townspeople—found their way into the private places of the castle."

"We'll have to wait," I said.

"Don't worry about me," Dahlia said. "I'm fine staying here as long as you need me to. As your new lady-in-waiting, I'm totally available to you as an artist and friend. Do you want to discuss color schemes or . . . ?"

"Not right now, Dahlia," I said.

"Hold on. New lady-in-waiting?" Eugene asked. "What happened to Miss Delightful?"

"Who?" Dahlia asked.

"He means Cassandra," I explained.

"Did you finally give her the axe?" Eugene asked.

"What axe?" I said. "She has plenty of axes of her own."

"It's an expression," Dahlia said. "He means, did you ask her not to be your lady-in-waiting anymore."

"No!" I said.

"What happened?" Eugene asked.

I took a deep breath, closed my eyes, and thought. The last time I told Eugene something about Cass it was a disaster for her.

"Rapunzel? What's going on? Is Cass in danger?" Eugene asked.

"She might be," I said. After all, she'd made a rash decision. "Cass is gone." This was an emergency. And anyway, it wasn't going to take long for everyone else to figure out she was missing.

"What do you mean?" Eugene asked, taking my hands in his.

"She was really angry and she stormed off. I'm not here to judge," Dahlia said. "But Cassandra is pretty high-strung."

"Darling, are you in there?" my mother called from the other side of the door. "I have the captain of the guard with me. We need to talk to you."

"Under the bed," Eugene whispered to Dahlia.

CHAPTER THIRTY-TWO

She smiled, pleased to be breaking the rules—in the tradition of artists, I guessed—and then slunk under my bed.

"I'm here," I said.

My mother, father, and the captain of the guard entered.

"Hi, Eugene. You look nice. Rapunzel, what is going on, dear?" Mom said.

"What do you mean?" I asked, hoping my mother wouldn't see straight through me, which of course she did.

"There's a problem," Mom said, getting down to business. "We're looking for information, darling." Mom sat next to me and placed her hands over mine. "Cassandra never showed up to the bake-off. She's missing."

"I know," I said.

"Why didn't you tell me?" Mom asked.

"She wanted me to let her go," I said. Mom's eyes darkened with concern. A bubble rose in my throat. "She said she just wasn't happy here. I didn't want her to feel trapped."

"Not happy here?" Mom asked, shaking her head as she squeezed my hand. "But I thought you two were getting along so beautifully."

"We were," I said.

"I don't mean to appear insensitive, Your Highness," the captain said. "But I need to gather as much information as possible as quickly as I can. Where did she go? When did she leave?"

"I don't know any of that," I told them. "The last time I saw her was this afternoon and she told me that if I wanted her to be happy, I shouldn't follow her."

"Why didn't you come to get me?" Dad asked. "Rapunzel, we depend on you to be a responsible member of the royal family. We've lost valuable time."

"I'm sorry," I said, tears spilling down my cheeks. "I want Cass to find her destiny."

"I'll see you both outside," Mom said, signaling to my father and the captain. "And you, too, Eugene. I need some alone time with my daughter."

After they left the room, Mom put an arm around me. "You can tell me anything, sweetheart. What-ever happened, I won't say a word. Why was Cass unhappy?"

"She didn't want to be a lady-in-waiting, Mom. She wanted to be in the guard. And it's really hard to keep someone from what she wants, deep in her heart."

"That's true," she said. "You're a wise soul. Wisdom, you know, is the most important quality for a queen to possess, because it affects everything she does and every life she touches."

"But I'm a terrible friend." I buried my face against Mom's shoulder.

"Why would you say that, Rapunzel?" Mom asked.

"I told Eugene something I shouldn't have," I said. "Something that Cassandra asked me to keep private."

"I see," Mom said with a thoughtful nod. "Everyone makes mistakes. You're a very good friend. I've seen it in the way you care for everyone in this castle. I've seen it in the way you've treated Cassandra—joining her in her interests, I presume."

"Wait. You *knew* about that?" I asked.

"It shows in your flower arrangements," Mom said, pointing to my latest attempt at floral decor. "This doesn't exactly look like the result of careful study."

A slight grin let me know that she wasn't chiding me. "But flower arrangements are the least of our worries right now, Rapunzel—we need to find Cassandra. It's dangerous for a solo traveler. You should know that better than anyone."

"What do you mean, dangerous?" I asked, my stomach tightening. "How dangerous?"

"Bandits, thieves, ruffians," Mom said. "I hate to say this, but I'd even feel better if the two of you were together. You're our best hope of finding her, Rapunzel. You must have some idea of where she went—some clue."

"I don't," I said. "She was so determined, and so angry. . . ."

"When we're really upset, it's difficult to remember the important details. Why don't you write in your diary? Sometimes when the mind relaxes, the answers come. Your father and the captain are rushing you, but I believe with a little space, you might be able to give us the information we need to find her. In the meantime, we'll deploy some of our forces to begin the search."

"What about the ball?"

"This is more important. I can always say that you're ill. Monsieur LaFleur is leading everyone in a most unconventional dance—but everyone seems to be enjoying it."

I nodded. She kissed my forehead and stood up as I reached for my diary.

"Oh, and there was an old book in the hallway," Mom said. She left for a moment and then returned with it. "I wondered if it was yours, since you are such a voracious reader. Someone must have left it for you. Or did you drop it by accident?"

In the chaos, I'd forgotten about the book Cass had been holding! "Yes," I said, taking it from her. "Cass brought it for me."

"*The Lost Language: Insights into Saporian Myths and Legends?*" Mom asked.

"We love history," I said, holding it to my chest.

"You girls fascinate me," Mom said.

Once Mom was out of the room, Dahlia crawled out from under the bed. I hadn't remembered she was there.

"Did you overhear all that?" I asked, wincing.

She nodded. "I kind of couldn't help it."

"Maybe I should have followed her," I said to Dahlia, gazing out the window as though I might actually catch sight of Cassandra. It was darker than usual and the trees cast odd shadows. "Do you think I did the right thing?"

"You have to listen to your heart." She sighed, pulling her ringlets behind her ears. "You have to trust your intuition. Judging yourself is the worst thing you can do, as an artist and a person."

Her words had the ring of truth, but I still couldn't believe them. Not while Cass was in danger.

Owl appeared at the window. I opened it, and he settled on the sill.

"You have an owl *and* a lizard?" Dahlia asked.

"He's Cassandra's," I said, holding out my hand to pet him. He placed Cassandra's friendship bracelet in my hand. It was broken! Had she ripped it off in anger? As if he could read my mind, Owl hooted once, communicating distress rather than anger. I gripped the bracelet and brought it into the light. It was covered with the emerald green moss that I'd only ever seen in one place—the path to the lagoon.

Cassandra was on her way there—and she was in danger. I felt it in my gut. And just as Dahlia had said, I knew I had to trust my intuition for what to do next.

"Dahlia," I said, turning to face her. She was setting up her easel and paints.

"If I'm going to be here a while, I might as well get some work done, right?" she asked.

"Dahlia, sometimes I think the world is our canvas and we're the brushes, right?"

"Sure," she said.

"Here's the situation. I'm going to go after my friend—but I need to go alone. My mother may come and check on me later, and I'm wondering if you might sleep in my bed with the covers around you?" I asked.

"Like performance art?" she asked.

"Exactly," I said.

"That won't be a problem," Dahlia said.

"Perfect," I said, turning down my sheets. "Can you start right now?"

I snuck out of my room and quietly knocked on Eugene's door.

"I'm going to find her," I said when he answered the door.

"What?" he asked. "Rapunzel, it's late. It's dark. I can't let you go alone."

"Eugene, I trusted you when I told you the truth about how I left the kingdom the night my hair grew back. Now I need you to trust me that I know what I'm doing. I won't be wandering aimlessly. I know where to find her."

"Where?" he asked.

"I can't tell you that," I said. "I just need you to trust me."

"Rapunzel—your safety—" he started.

"Eugene." I took him by the shoulders and looked

deep into his eyes. "My whole life I've been told to stay inside for my safety. Now something—*someone*— needs me. Sometimes the most dangerous thing to do is to *not* take action. I need to help my friend."

"I trust you," he said.

"Thank you," I said. I could feel in my bones that he believed me. "Dahlia is in my bed, pretending to be me. I know that if my mother sees me sleeping, she won't disturb me."

"I'll do my best to distract them. Thank you for telling me the truth," Eugene said.

"Always," I said.

"Now go, find your friend. She needs you," he said, and embraced me. "Keep this with you." He kissed me sweetly and my heart swelled with love and courage.

Knowing that the book about Saporia might offer some clue, I tucked it inside my satchel. Then I wrapped my hair around my window ledge and lowered myself to the ground. The earth was cold and rough beneath my bare feet.

I looked up at the sky. The full moon was hidden in shadow except for a faint line around its perimeter. Something flew low and close by my head. I stifled a shriek and ducked before I realized it was Owl. He hooted and arched upward.

"Owl, what are you trying to tell me?" I whispered. "Does that mean I should go or not?"

He soared into the distance. Thinking that he wouldn't leave me if it was dangerous, I made a run for it, sliding behind a tree as soon as I passed the guards' stations. My heart was beating loudly and rapidly, and cold sweat pricked the back of my neck. The only other times I'd done this, I'd been with Cass. Now I was going to have to get there on my own. I searched the sky for guidance, but Owl was long gone.

"I'm on my way, Cass," I said, hoping my words might somehow reach her. "You're not alone."

I hitched up my skirt and, staying close to the shadows, ran through the trees. I was used to running barefoot, and I felt a sense of purpose so strong that I moved with the speed and grace of a fox. I reached the path in what felt like record time. Now I just needed to get to the other side before anything happened to my friend.

33

CASSANDRA

"**M**arco!" I said, twisting my body to get a glimpse of my attacker's face.

"Pleasure to see you again," he said as he dug his knee into my back. I bit back a cry of pain. Owl had disappeared.

"Where's my sword?" I asked.

"Consider it disposed of," he said, applying more pressure to my spine. "Keep in mind, I could do a lot more damage to a wisp of a girl like yourself, but then you wouldn't be much use, would you?"

"Rapunzel isn't with me," I said. "I have no money. Doesn't Xavier pay you?"

"What do you think I am? A common thief? It's

not money I'm after, you stupid girl. It's the lagoon," he said. He grabbed the knife from my belt and pressed it to my neck.

"What lagoon?" I asked. It was a good thing he thought I was stupid. He'd somehow found the pathway, but he wasn't expecting the gulch—the wall of rock that hid the lagoon. What had Raps and I missed there? What exactly was he after?

"Don't play ignorant with me," Marco said.

"Oh, you mean the lagoon in the poem?" I said. How could I get the knife in my boot? If my ankle hadn't been wounded, I might have had a chance of kicking him off me; but with my injury, my only weapon was my wit.

"The one that I've spent my entire life studying. You and the princess have been there and I know it," he said. "I stole the original book from your satchel. Then I heard you discussing it during your matchmaking session." A realization came to me: he must have been the lute player hidden in the shadows! "And when I saw Herz Der Sonne's spearhead in your possession," he continued, "I finally had the proof I needed. When I went back to Rapunzel's room to search for more clues, I realized you were missing the key piece of information. I assume Xavier passed along the book to you?"

"Huh?" I asked, playing dumb.

"Of course he did, or you wouldn't be here," he said.

"What book?"

"Don't lie to me, girl!" Marco said, pressing the knife to my neck. His breath smelled like old onions and dirty socks. "I even bookmarked the page for you to ensure you'd come tonight. Imagine! Two silly little girls did most of the hard work for me with the discovery and translation of that poem."

"I have no idea what you're talking about," I said.

"Please. I know we're close. I'll be the most powerful man in Corona once I tap into the power of the lagoon. Forget the guard—I'll be the new *king*. This is my destiny," he hissed.

"Get off my friend," came a voice from above. Marco and I looked up.

It was Rapunzel, her dress torn at the elbows. She was high in a tree, balanced, and striking a fencer's aggressive lunge. She swung around a branch by her hair and, in a moment that took my breath away, kicked Marco in the head. He tumbled backward.

As he tried to reorient himself, I grabbed my

knife from his hand. Touching his skin made the hair on the back of my neck stand up.

"Repugnant imp!" Marco said.

"What is it you want, Marco?" Rapunzel asked. There was no trace of the peppy princess here. Rapunzel was in full warrior mode.

"He thinks the lagoon is real," I said to her, improvising. "He thinks you and I know where it is."

"We do!" Rapunzel said. Her grin was wide, but smirking. I'd never seen her smirk before.

"See how sweet your little friend is," Marco said, sneering at me. "Such a good princess, an obedient girl."

"Hold on. I thought I was a 'repugnant imp,'" Raps said, hands on her hips, eyebrows arched.

"No, no, no. You misunderstood. That's *her*. You, my pet, are an angelic sprite. So willing to cooperate. A fine young lady, indeed. Must be that good breeding of yours. Tell dear Marco all about the lagoon."

What was she up to? "Uh, Rapunzel—" I started.

"We *are* at the lagoon!" Rapunzel said, spinning around in the green moss. Marco's lip turned up in a semi-snarl. "Watch as I swim!"

Rapunzel completely committed to the fantasy.

"'When on a winter eve we met, our truth was but a glimmer,'" she said, prancing on the moss. She stroked the boulders and added, "'The moon shone extra bright; fortune far beneath did shimmer.'" Then, as if seeing a vision, she made a visor with her hand and shouted, "'Here was Corona built, amidst ebbing fear and flowing doubt. When voices clash and metal strikes, the light within tamps out.'"

We locked eyes and I stifled a giggle.

She, however, stayed in character as she knelt by a patch of plain daisies. "See? Here are the glimmering jewels! I just love how the moonlight makes them sparkle."

"What nonsense is this?" Marco asked. "Are you quite mad?"

"I know!" Rapunzel said, refusing to answer his question. "You're looking for the ancient power. The one we were asking Xavier about." She smiled as though she were positively bursting with joy. "That's harder to find, of course. But I'll show you if you ask politely."

"Uh . . . please?" Marco said, totally confused.

"That and a coin will get you a cup of coffee," Raps said with a grin.

I had to laugh aloud. I just couldn't keep it in! She'd remembered the expression I'd taught her so many months ago.

"Pretty please . . ." Marco said. Raps gestured for more. "With a candied plum on top?"

"I do love candied plums . . ." Rapunzel said. She rustled in the bush and then said, "Here!" She handed him a rock.

"This is nothing but a rock," Marco said. "What fanciful delusions am I partaking in? Are you having a fit?"

"Watch out for the golden fish!" I said as a few fireflies buzzed past.

"Golden fish, how lucky! I'll catch them for our supper!" Rapunzel said, opening her palms and following the bright buzzing creatures. She cupped her hands, just missing one. "Whoops!"

Above, Owl cruised in joyful circles.

"The lagoon you've been speaking to Xavier about is just in your little heads?" Marco asked.

"Inspired by the poem, imagined by us," Rapunzel declared, slinging an arm around my neck. "I don't know if you've heard, but my head is kind of in the clouds."

"Brilliantly so," I said. "Gives her an incredible view."

"Isn't it wonderful, Marco?" Raps said, stepping forward and spreading her arms in an expansive gesture. "The lagoon is wherever you want it to be, *whenever* you want it to be."

"That phrase you mentioned to Xavier was the most prescient detail of all. *Ackoui rescede o oure treasure, ligaro comme an embrace, nayo dixie que sejir disturbe.* That didn't come from your heads," Marco said in disbelief. "Years of painstaking study are the only reason I know its importance. It's written on the walls, isn't it?"

"I guess I'm a quicker study," Rapunzel said.

"It's in the ancient documents," I said, jumping in, "which she's been researching like crazy. You know us 'silly girls'; we get obsessed with stories. Especially this one. Look at her. She has seventy-foot long hair, bare feet, and a chameleon she talks to like a person."

"I'm a free spirit with a lot of time on my hands," Rapunzel said.

"Then why the secrecy?" Marco asked. "Why are you here in the middle of the night?"

"I was running away," I said. "My friend came to find me."

"Friend?" Rapunzel asked hesitantly. We both paused. This was about more than Marco.

CHAPTER THIRTY-THREE

"The best," I said. Then I knelt in the mud and scooped up a handful of dirt. "Would you like some of our lagoon cake?"

"With coffee?" Rapunzel asked, dripping mud on top of it.

"No, thank you," Marco said. "Though I'm going to make sure you two don't breathe a word about this. If you think I'm going to let you make a fool of me, guess again." He whipped one of the new daggers from Xavier's shop from his waistcoat—a hidden weapon. "I'd never hurt a princess, but no one would miss a lady-in-waiting. I'll take a toe as a warning."

"Oh, I don't know if you want to do that," I said, jumping back just in time.

"Why not?" asked Marco.

"There's a Winged Beast on the loose," I said. Rapunzel and I made eye contact. I whispered, "I'll do the aerial portion."

"But . . ." Rapunzel said. "There's no protection."

"I trust you. You've got both feet on the ground. Anyway, my ankle is hurt."

"I didn't come here to suffer humiliation," Marco said, lunging for me.

"No, you just came here to try to take over Corona," Rapunzel said. On the count of three,

Rapunzel threw me in the air. I knocked Marco down, leaving him unconscious, and landed in Rapunzel's arms.

"We did it!" she said, turning me upright and squeezing me. "We did the Winged Beast!"

"I can't believe it," I said. I'd always dreamed of this accomplishment, but had never imagined it would be a reality—that I would be able to work with someone the way I had with her. I couldn't stop grinning. *The Winged Beast!*

We stood there, breathless, our eyes fixed on the unconscious Marco. Rapunzel knelt and took his pulse.

"He'll be all right when he comes to," she said. "Let's take him far away, so he won't know where he is."

"Owl, can you get Fidella for us?" I asked.

"Fidella will ride him straight out of Corona," Rapunzel said. "Who knows where he'll wake up, but he won't be back anytime soon."

"We're safe," I said, kneeling on the moss.

"We're *all* safe," she said, looking up at the thin circle in the sky, which was the hidden moon.

34

RAPUNZEL

"We need to get to the lagoon," Cass said, standing on one foot and leaning against a tree. We'd found her sword in the bushes near where Marco had attacked her, and she'd tried to convince me that she was perfectly fine. But I could see the pain in her eyes, even though they were also brimming with excitement. "Did you bring the book I left behind?"

"Yes—it's in here!" I said. I pulled it out of my satchel. *"The Lost Language: Insights into Saporian Myths and Legends.* We can figure out what Marco was talking about. But safety first! I need to tend to your foot. It's swollen to the size of my frying pan."

"I already wrapped it," Cass said.

"With a napkin?" I asked. She shrugged. "With all the guard training we've done, including extensive first aid, you should know that a sprained ankle needs more support than a napkin."

"I didn't have anything else to wrap it in," Cassandra said.

"Hmmm," I said, looking around. I spotted a jagged rock. I picked up the cloak I'd tossed aside before the Winged Beast took flight, and I used the sharp edge of the rock to tear a hole in it. I ripped a swath of material free.

"I didn't know you had that in you," Cassandra said, genuinely stunned.

"Excuse me, but I just performed the Winged Beast," I said. "In case you didn't know, that's the ultimate feat of a great warrior." Cassandra laughed. Somewhere nearby, the animals of the night were chattering. We froze as a family of skunks trotted past us, then burst into more laughter as they disappeared into the woods behind us.

"That'll be a few hours' worth of sewing for me," she said, gesturing to my torn cloak. "And we both know how much I adore sewing."

"Let's apply some pressure," I said. "Does this hurt?"

CHAPTER THIRTY-FOUR

"Just a little," she said.

"Maybe we shouldn't go to the lagoon tonight," I said, tightening the fabric. "Maybe we need to wait until you make a full recovery."

"Are you kidding?" Cassandra asked. "Raps, you have to be crazy if you think I'm just going to ignore—"

"Just teasing!" I said, laughing as I tucked the edge of the fabric into the layers to secure the bandage. Then I gave her the lantern and the book. "You're way more gullible than you'd ever admit! Go ahead. Read."

"There's a whole chapter on 'The Lost Lagoon.' English was not the first language of the poet. It was Saporian. In that language, 'precious stones' does not translate to jewels or gems; it refers to the rock slabs that were commonly used as writing tablets."

"We were never looking for stone tablets!" I said. "But I still can't believe we missed them. We've searched every corner of that lagoon!"

"There's more," Cass said. "Listen." She began to read aloud: "'When the moon is full, forces pull the ground at the bottom of the lagoon in polar directions, revealing a hidden space in the lagoon's floor. However, it's only during a lunar eclipse that the hidden space becomes apparent, as that's when the light of the phosphorescent creatures provides adequate visibility.'"

"We don't need moonlight, we need a lunar eclipse!" I said, staring up at the sky. The moon was a ghost of itself, outlined in a bright silver light. "That's why Marco thought we'd come tonight! Let's go!" The potential for discovery lit a fire within me. I took a deep breath of the chilly night air and offered Cassandra my hand. "So, if you're planning on repairing my cape, does that mean you aren't running away anymore?"

"Is everyone looking for me?" she asked, not committing to an answer but leaning on me nevertheless. I nodded. She winced. "You told them I ran away?"

"They noticed you were gone without me having to tell them," I said, guiding us toward the gulch. "You had an important role as a taster at the bake-off."

"Yeah, yeah. I'm sure the bakers survived. Are they looking for you, too?" she asked as she hobbled along.

"Not yet," I said. "At least I don't think so. Dahlia is lying in my bed, posing as me. And Eugene will distract them if he needs to."

"Do they know where we are?" Cassandra asked.

"No," I said. We had just reached the steep rock wall. I faced her and looked directly in her eyes. "And by the way, Dahlia was just helping me make something. I didn't even really tell her what it was. I just needed some supplies."

"Really?" she asked.

"Yes," I said. "Who knew you'd be so sensitive about friendship bracelets?" I winked.

"Ugh! Not you, too! No winking!" she said.

I laughed, wrapping my hair around her and carrying her over the rock barrier, then slowly and steadily lowered us into the gulch. The narrow walls magnified the lantern's light. It cast a warm glow around us, as though the moon itself accompanied us.

"Why didn't you just tell me you were buying supplies?" she asked.

"You wouldn't give me a chance," I said. "And she was helping me with a present for *you*—if you must know."

"What present?" Cassandra asked.

"You're just going to have to wait and see," I said. "You were right, by the way. I need to be more careful about who I invite back to my room. There's a lot at stake—more than I realized."

"And you were a great warrior today," Cass said. "You *do* have good instincts."

We waded around the last corner of the gulch, and then I climbed over the final ridge. I let down my hair so Cass could climb up it. We were both stunned into absolute silence when we came across the lagoon.

The starfish, which we'd seen so many times before, were lit up like miniature lanterns, illuminating the very bottom of the lagoon—even the tiny nooks and crannies—in a way that sunlight and moonlight couldn't do. It was only in the pitch black that they shone so brightly.

"Do you see them?" I asked her.

"The stones under the jewels," she said. "The tablets!"

"Let's go get them," I said, placing the lantern on a rock.

"I can't put pressure on my ankle, but I can swim," Cassandra said.

We stripped down to our bloomers and camisoles and dove into the water.

Using the starfish as our guides, we freed the tablets from the bottom of the lagoon and then swam back up to the surface. Cassandra and I each held one and then, realizing they had once been a single stone, fit them together like a puzzle.

"'Let there be only love here,'" Cassandra read, hovering over the tablet with the lantern. "And it's signed."

"'Shampanier, poet and general,'" I said. "Shampanier is the author of the poem! This is a love poem—I was right! It's a love poem about Shampanier and Herz Der Sonne!"

"What does the other half say?" Cassandra asked.

I pulled out the Saporian dictionary and did my best to translate. "It is here that we made our vow to join our kingdoms. Peace is our treasure. When opposites come together in the name of love and goodness, despite their differences, they manifest the ultimate power. As long as this land is not disturbed nor will our country's peace be."

"They may have used some gems for the ceremony, but the treasure is peace," Cassandra said.

"They had a secret wedding here!" I said, unable to contain my enthusiasm. "That's what the altar is for."

"Look!" Cassandra said, turning the interlocking stones over. "There's more on the back." It was in English. She read aloud: "'If anyone shall make this discovery, hold it close. Sacrifice an object to bind you to this place, as we rulers have sacrificed our weapons. Take this vow: herein lies our treasure, bonded with an embrace, let it not be disturbed.'"

"I was right, too!" Cassandra said. "This has to be where they met when they wanted to be alone. It's also where they worked out their politics, and surrendered their weapons."

"The spearhead," I said. "It was Herz Der Sonne's! This explains why half of the notes are written in English and half are written in Saporian."

"I feel like we're a part of something major," Cassandra said.

"I feel like I'm a part of Corona," I said. "Maybe I do belong here."

"Of course you do," Cass said, sounding surprised. "You're the princess."

"This is the first time that I feel like it," I said, and the truth of the words calmed my heart. "Solving this mystery was my true coronation."

She considered this. "So, what are we going to sacrifice?"

"Our bracelets," I said.

"That makes sense, because we found the stones here," Cassandra said.

CHAPTER THIRTY-FOUR

"They should be returned to sacred ground,"
I said. "And anyway, this is the only place they
sparkle."

I scurried up the rocks to my satchel, handed
Cassandra her bracelet, and then presented my
wrist for her to untie mine.

"Herein lies our treasure, bonded with an
embrace, let it not be disturbed," we said in unison,
and then we tossed our bracelets into the lagoon.

"Okay, so I know that you're not into touchy-feely
stuff," I said. "But I pretty much think we *have* to
hug right now."

"Okay, fine," Cass said. And we did. "Listen, Raps,
you let me do my thing by practicing the Winged
Beast. I know you have to do your things, too. Like
telling Eugene what you have to tell him. Or making a new friend. We both have destinies to find.
I wouldn't be a good lady-in-waiting if I held you
back from yours."

"Cass, that is the sweetest, kindest, loveliest
thing that anyone—" I started. Before I could go
on, Cassandra jumped, taking me with her. We
screamed with delight as we dropped into the
water.

35

CASSANDRA

"What on earth are all these guards doing out?" I asked. We crouched as we hid behind a cluster of trees at the edge of the castle grounds. My ankle throbbed. Wisps of fog were in the autumn air, chilling us. Judging by the bruised color of the sky, it was about four-thirty in the morning.

"They're looking for you," Rapunzel said.

"Impossible. They're here for the festival," I said, wondering how we were going to make it past the guards and get into our rooms undetected.

"The festival ended hours ago," Raps said.

Owl, who we'd sent to scope out the scene, landed

on my arm. "What do you say, Owl? Do they know Raps is outside of the castle?"

Owl ruffled his feathers and hooted quietly. "That's a 'no,' " I said.

"Oh, nice! My Dahlia plan worked!" Rapunzel said.

"So all this security is for me?" I asked quietly, not really intending to pose the question aloud. It was hard for me to comprehend that so many people would care about my absence.

"Of course it is," Rapunzel said, taking my arm. "Cass, don't you see? So many people care about you. Me, your father, my parents, Friedborg . . ."

"Friedborg?" I asked, cocking an eyebrow. "Raps. Give me a break."

"I'm sure she was concerned! And I know you may not believe me, but Eugene was worried, too."

"You're right," I said, pushing a strand of hair behind my ear. "I don't believe you."

"I know he rubs you the wrong way, but Eugene is not as bad as you think. He's pretty wonderful, actually. He's kind and helpful, and sweet and handsome. . . ."

"Okay, okay, okay! I get your point!" I said.

"And anyway, you're the only other person in all of Corona who knows about the ancient power,"

Raps said. "You belong here as much as I do. And you know you can't argue with me about that."

She's right, I thought. And that wasn't something I could usually admit. I noticed her bare feet were covered in dirt.

"Hey, when you're queen and I'm captain of the guard, do you think we can outlaw high heels?" I asked.

She laughed. "I don't know about outlawing them, but we can definitely set a trend."

Owl hooted, alerting me that someone was approaching. I yanked on Rapunzel's arm, pulling her down into the shadows.

I whispered, "Right now, we focus on getting inside. Or at least getting *you* inside."

"What do you mean? I'm not going without you!" Rapunzel said.

"Raps, if Owl is right and no one knows that you're gone, we have to make sure you're back in your chambers as soon as possible and that you make it there safely and quietly. It'll be better for all of us."

"What about you?" Raps asked.

"I'm going to surrender myself," I said. "Whatever the punishment is for running away, I should take it."

CHAPTER THIRTY-FIVE

"We're a team. Let's surrender together," Raps said.

"No—if we do that, the punishment will be worse," I said. "You have to know that by now. Plus, your hair is wet. There will be too many questions."

Rapunzel considered for a moment and then nodded. "So what's the plan?"

"If I create a distraction by surrendering myself, the guard force will be decreased," I said. "And then you dart over to the garden below your window and wait until the coast is clear. I'll send Owl to warn Pascal. He can open the window—"

"And then I'll use my hair to climb back into my room," Rapunzel said. She bit her lip. "Dahlia's still there, I think."

"We'll have to deal with her later," I said. "When dawn comes, maybe your 'dreamboat' Eugene can secretly escort her back to the market."

"He'd do it for me," Raps said. "And for you."

"I'll believe it when I see it. Are you ready for this?" I asked.

Raps nodded. She flattened herself against the earth. Then I stood up and walked toward the castle, ready to face the world.

36

RAPUNZEL

"I think I'm starting to get a feel for what it was like for you to be locked in a tower for eighteen years!" Dahlia said when, after climbing the length of my hair, I crawled through my window and collapsed on the floor. Dahlia wasn't lying in my bed pretending to be me, asleep. She was busy at work, decorating a slab of wood.

Pascal pointed to her and rolled his eyes with exasperation. He had clearly had enough of Dahlia.

"Technically, it's only been a day," I said, pulling my hair up behind me with great effort. If seventy feet of hair was a lot to carry around, seventy feet of *wet* hair was a ton. "I get that you're going a little stir-crazy, but I'm not sure that's an accurate comparison." I tumbled onto the floor as I pulled the last of my hair inside.

"Maybe you're right," she said with a sigh. "As an artist, I don't always think of time and space in a linear fashion. And I'm not sure you do, either."

"What do you mean?" I asked. "And, um, what are you doing?"

"I'm transferring one of your sketches to a piece of wood using special glue."

"Oh . . ."

"Your style doesn't abide by rules. Take this, for example," she said, holding up one of my sketches of Cass. It had started as a drawing, but then later I'd added paint. "I get a feeling from the picture without knowing the time or even the place. From your brushstrokes and composition, pure emotion comes across."

"Really?" I asked, gazing at the half-finished portrait of the two of us.

"There's a lot of movement," Dahlia said. "It's vibrant."

"That's Cass," I said

"That's not just Cass, though," Dahlia said. "See, it's also the way you feel when you're with her, right?"

"Wow," I said. Even though I'd spent countless hours drawing and painting, fully absorbed in the process, I'd never really talked to anyone about it before.

"In my mind, this all relates to time and space," Dahlia said.

"I think I get what you're saying," I said. "I mean, when I'm with Cass, and when I'm painting, time does move differently."

"You are a seriously amazing princess," Dahlia said. "But I really need to get out of here. My spirit is, like, itching." She gestured toward the wood. "Do you mind if I let this piece dry here while I get back to my cart?"

"Sure," I said. "Where's the wood from?"

"It was one of your bookshelves. You don't mind, do you?" Dahlia said.

"I guess not?" I said, glancing at the bookshelves Eugene and I had planned and that the royal carpenter had built, now missing the bottom shelf. Dahlia had stacked up the books that were on the bottom shelf in an artful way. They actually looked pretty, lying horizontally where the others above them were positioned vertically. And she'd clearly done it with care—the stacks were color-coordinated. "Maybe next time you could ask me, though, okay?"

"Okay," Dahlia said, closing her suitcase of supplies and walking toward my door. "Though, you know, sometimes you need to ruin something in order to make it what it really wants to be."

"Wait!" I said. She froze, and I could tell the sharpness of my voice had startled her. "Sorry, Dahlia, but we're still going to have to sneak you out of here." I peeked out the window. There were only a few guards, and they were all by the drawbridge, crowding around. Owl circled above. I knew the crowd had gathered for Cassandra's return. She had turned herself in. A sense of ease filled me. Cassandra was back, and she wasn't going anywhere. "Okay. The coast is clear. You can't just waltz down the hall, though. You're going to have to exit by window."

"No problem. If you could just let this piece dry overnight and then bring it by the market, that would be great. I'd really like to display it," Dahlia said. Pascal shook his head, totally fed up. Dahlia had turned out to be pretty demanding. But she had an interesting point of view. Especially about art.

"I'll do my best," I said.

The sun was starting to rise, peeking above the distant hills with red rays.

"Hey, have you ever used hair as a material before?" I asked.

"No," she said.

"Well, you're about to descend it as if it were a rope. That should give you a new perspective," I said.

And once again, I let down my hair.

CASSANDRA

I joined the royal family for tea the next day, after the Hervanians had said their good-byes. Evidently, Marie had had such a fun time at the festival—the fencing demonstration and Monsieur LaFleur's revolution dance being the highlights—that they'd insisted on coming back for the next big Coronan festival. I would not be looking forward to that, but I had bigger fish to fry at the moment.

I arrived to the royal tea promptly at three o'clock. The king, queen, Rapunzel, and Eugene were there. I didn't see why he needed to be included, but then again, I never did

"You certainly gave us a scare last night, my dear," Queen Arianna said to me when I limped inside. My ankle was still tender.

"I'm sorry," I said, curtsying as well as I could.

"When Rapunzel told us that you had run away, we were devastated," Queen Arianna said, pouring the tea as Friedborg arrived with a tray of crumpets.

"Apologies," I reiterated.

When I'd surrendered myself, a legion of guards had lifted me up and chanted a victory cry. They had cheered so loudly my ears were still ringing. Moments later, my father had embraced me with tears in his eyes. It was the first time that I'd seen my father cry. And then a written invitation for tea had come from the queen herself first thing in the morning.

"Cassandra, dear, you know that you have a place here in Corona," Queen Arianna said, placing her warm hand over mine. At that moment, I couldn't help noticing that she and Rapunzel had identical hands—long fingers, prominent knuckles, and strong palms. Raps, seated on the other side of me, squeezed my other hand.

"A very important place," the king said, dabbing his mouth with a napkin. "We know your official title is lady-in-waiting, but because of your special skill set . . ."

"Your extraordinary fighting skills," Rapunzel piped up.

"Because you are *you*," Queen Arianna said, getting to the heart of it, "we also think of you as Rapunzel's protector."

"Of course, I'm *also* Rapunzel's protector," Eugene said. "Some might even say the *main* one." Eugene's eyes widened and I bit back a smile. I knew Rapunzel was probably pinching him under the table.

"Um, I don't know if anyone here has noticed, but I'm pretty good at protecting myself," Rapunzel said.

"I've noticed," I said. I turned to the queen. "Your daughter is very strong."

"No one doubts your abilities, Rapunzel," Queen Arianna said. "But in this world, we need to look out for each other. A team is stronger than one person."

"I know," I said, locking eyes with Rapunzel. I couldn't help thinking of the words on the tablets in the lagoon. "Which is why I'm especially sorry that I ran away. I had a moment where I thought my destiny was to leave."

"The call of destiny is a strong one, to be certain," Queen Arianna said. "I heard it myself at your age. At several points in life, we feel the need to search—and perhaps the desire to wander. If our lives were laid out before us in neat maps, how would we grow? If we didn't yearn or question, what would happen to our souls?"

I shook my head, speechless.

"And yet, ironically, surrendering to your destiny, the one you feel deep in your soul, is the bravest act," the king said.

"You belong here, my dear girl," Queen Arianna said.

"With us," Rapunzel added. And I knew they were right.

38

RAPUNZEL

"**H**ere is the picture I was going to give you before you left," I said, presenting the book-shaped portrait to Cassandra after dinner.

"Is that me?" she asked, studying the sketch.

"Yes," I said. "This is what I was working on when you decided to run away."

"I like it," Cassandra said. "Do you think I could help you finish it?"

"You want to do that?" I asked, surprised. Cass had never before seemed interested in my artwork.

"You helped me so much with the Winged Beast. I think it's time I learn a little more about art. I bet if I study hard enough, I could learn as much as Dahlia," she said.

"I don't want you to be like Dahlia," I said, setting up my easel and opening the jars of paint. "Dahlia has a lot of great qualities, and she knows a ton about art, but I'd rather hang out with you— at least, most of the time."

Cass didn't even try to hide her smile. I handed her a jar with a tight lid and she opened it with ease. I realized then that even though she may not ever ask for it, she needed some reassurance.

"You know," I said, "your maps are works of art."

"They're practical documents," Cass said.

"They're both!" I said. "Why don't you go get them?"

She did, and as soon as she returned, I continued. "I was thinking that if I combined your map of the lagoon with my portraits, we could create something truly unique and beautiful."

"I guess it's kind of dangerous to have a map to secret places just lying around," Cassandra said. "What if it fell into the wrong hands?"

Something that Dahlia had said had inspired me. *Sometimes you need to ruin something in order to make it what it really wants to be.* I took out some sewing sheers and cut through the canvas with our portraits on them.

"What are you doing?" Cassandra asked.

"I'm making art," I said proudly. I used some paint to place the pictures of us on the map, right in the place where the lagoon was. "See, it's us. At the lagoon.

"Here," I said, and I handed Cassandra a paintbrush.

"What do I do with it?" she asked, holding it as though it were a foreign object—one that might bite her.

"Draw what you see with your heart," I said. She wrinkled her nose at me. I laughed. "Okay, fine. Just paint something from the lagoon."

She dipped her brush in yellow and drew an outline around our bodies.

"Is that the light from the shimmering gems?" I asked. She nodded.

I mixed the blue with a dollop of black and swirled the colors around to create a shade of midnight. Then I painted over the map. Cassandra gasped.

"The lagoon needs to be kept a secret to honor our friendship," I said as I covered her detailed lines and precise measurements with thick paint.

"And protect the kingdom," she said, taking her own brush to the canvas.

The fire crackled in the fireplace. And we worked until I felt in my gut that the artwork was done. The map was completely disguised, but our portraits were outlined in gold. It looked as though we were dancing through the air—together and free.